EERIE CHECK IN

MYSTIC INN MYSTERIES

STEPHANIE DAMORE

PINK SAPPHIRE PRESS

To Libby,
For your love and light

CHAPTER ONE

Crash! The flatscreen television Benny, the contractor, was installing above the fireplace smashed into a million pieces across the floor. I jumped, splashing my cup of coffee down the front of my blouse and onto my leather sandals.

"Ope! Sorry about that," Benny called down to us.

Aunt Thelma waved the contractor's remark away. "We're fine!" she sang back before innocently turning around to face me.

A mixture of glass and black plastic littered the floor. I closed my eyes and took a steadying breath. The inn's renovation was a nightmare, and I couldn't even blame it on our resident ghost, Percy the Poltergeist. First, the adhesive for the tile floors hadn't held. I could feel the tiles shifting under my feet, just waiting to be ripped out and replaced once more. After that, the new furniture went missing somewhere around Biloxi, Mississippi (if you could trust the shipping updates).

And now, none of the second-floor guest rooms had working bathrooms. Benny's crew had ripped out shower surrounds and toilets only to learn that the new ones were on backorder.

"Is he okay up there?" I side-eyed the older man balancing precariously on the top of the ladder, inspecting his handiwork, or lack thereof, while I dabbed the coffee stain off my blouse. It was pointless. I needed to change and treat the stain before it set in. Just another task to add to my to-do list. My stress level was dangerously high, and if I weren't careful, Aunt Thelma would insist I down a potion, or worse, raise her wand to "cure" me. I could admit that I was a witch now, but that didn't mean I wanted to be magicked. I saw what happened to the last guy.

"Oh, he's fine," Aunt Thelma glanced at the contractor over her shoulder with a shrug, sounding much too blasé.

I looked skeptical. The last thing we needed was someone getting hurt. Around us, workers buzzed about, cutting new shelving and switching the overhead lighting to LED bulbs. I kept my voice low, "Do you think we should hire someone else?" It wasn't the first time I'd expressed my concerns. I knew Benny was an old friend of my aunt's, but his project management skills were non-existent and this was a big job.

"How can you say that? It's not his fault the grout didn't mix, and I'm the one who ordered the furniture."

"And the TV?" I watched as a worker cleaned up the mess with a big push broom.

"Well, that's just an accident. Things will sort themselves out, you'll see."

I didn't have nearly the same optimism Aunt Thelma did. The fall festival was at the end of the week, the inn was booked solid for the event, and the renovations were not close to being done. I picked my coffee cup back up and looked down at my clipboard on the registration desk. The renovation schedule had been edited and re-edited. Red ink crossed out delivery dates only to have new dates come and go.

I looked back at my hodgepodge schedule. Today we were supposed to be staging—putting fresh flowers in the lobby, displaying artwork on the walls, and hanging the new welcome sign out front. Now, we'd be lucky if all the rooms had running water by the weekend.

"Hello?" The woman's cheerful voice echoed off the empty lobby.

I snapped my head up, and my mouth fell open. I couldn't believe who'd just walked in. It was a deer-in-headlights moment if I'd ever had one. I gave an inward groan at my rotten luck because that's officially what this was. I was convinced of it. Either that or we'd been cursed. I couldn't rule that out.

"Sophia? My word, it is you!" Aunt Thelma strode around the check-in counter and met her long-time friend and Silverlake's most famous resident with a fierce embrace.

Dread filled every inch of my being. I wished any other reservation would've checked in early.

Sophia Emerson was the perfect housewife of the witching world. She built an empire around the motto: Any Witch Can Do It!—referencing her numerous cookbooks and crafting shows. Sophia believed that if you were a witch, all you needed was the proper spell and a healthy dose of self-esteem, and the world was your oyster shell. Now here she was, strolling into our disaster of an inn. My face flushed with embarrassment. I mentally calculated how much trouble I'd get into if I froze Sophia on the spot and used a memory charm to erase the last minute until I could figure out what to do with her. I grimaced, imagining Deputy Amber Reynolds hauling me away in handcuffs. A smile on her face. I looked down, noting the stain on my blouse, and turned a deeper shade of crimson if that was even possible.

"What on earth are you doing here? You're a few days early!" Aunt Thelma held her friend at arm's length. Unlike my heated complexion, Aunt Thelma's glowed in happiness from the surprise.

"My schedule cleared up at the last minute, so here I am. I hope that's okay?"

"Of course! It's just that the inn's not quite ready for visitors. But I'm sure Angelica has a solution. You remember my niece?"

"Hi, Sophia, nice to see you again." I held out my hand to shake hers.

Sophia replied with a firm grip as she pumped my hand up and down.

"I know I should've called, but Arthur insisted we surprise you." Sophia apologized again.

"Arthur's here?" Aunt Thelma looked over Sophia's head, trying to spot her husband.

"Well, not right this second. He's golfing with Mike. But he'll join us for dinner." Sophia paused and looked hesitantly around the lobby. "I mean...if that's okay." For the first time since walking in, doubt clouded her eyes. Taking in a disaster tended to do that to a person.

"It's not as bad as it looks," Aunt Thelma bristled. The look I shot my aunt suggested otherwise. "The patio's inviting as ever, and we can order takeout from the Simmering Spoon," Aunt Thelma continued, ignoring my hesitation. She was doing that a lot lately.

"Do they still serve those mussels? You know the ones I'm talking about." Sophia's eyes sparkled.

"With the white wine sauce and crusty bread?" Aunt Thelma added.

"Yes!" Sophia clapped her hands.

"They haven't changed the recipe since you wrote it thirty years ago," Aunt Thelma remarked.

"Hush now. Has it been that long?" Sophia appeared to calculate the dates in her head. "You were being generous," she said with a laugh.

A buzz saw punctuated the air, and thank heavens I still wasn't holding my coffee cup, or I would've dumped the whole thing down the front of me.

"Watch where you're cutting!" Benny yelled down at a worker. "I said fifteen inches, not twelve! Watch it!"

Sophia grimaced. "I can stay somewhere else.

Really, it's not a problem," she said once the saw stopped whirling.

"Oh, stop. We can make something work. Right, Angelica?"

It was my turn to do some mental math. "I don't have any suites, but there are two adjoining rooms down the hall. Would those work? They're lake view with a small patio and outdoor access." I couldn't hide the skepticism in my voice. Sophia was used to the best of the best. Penthouse suites with butlers at the waiting, not guest rooms turned storage closets. I wish I were exagerating, but it was a fact. Most of the ground-floor rooms were piled with boxes full of new duvets, drapes, and towels, waiting to be unpacked and used once the rooms were complete.

"Anything is fine, really," Sophia's words rang hollow. Maybe it was her wrinkle-free linen suit after a cross-country flight or her polished designer shoes, but I wasn't buying it.

Still, I played along. "I'm going to need a bit of time to get the rooms ready." And a bit of help. I wondered how hard it would be to conjure the boxes upstairs to my apartment and where I would store them once I did.

"Don't worry, I know just the spell," Aunt Thelma said under her breath while Sophia was distracted by the workmen.

"'This room has great bones. With the elevated ceiling and fireplace, I could see why you want to hang the television there." Sophia assessed the lobby as Benny re-attached the television bracket.

"Thanks. That was my idea." Previously the old boxy television sat in front of the lobby's two sofas. But with the addition of the stone fireplace surround and mantel, I thought lifting the television off the ground made the space feel bigger.

"Except if I'm not mistaken, that's limestone." Sophia pointed to the stone above the fireplace. "Good luck getting a TV to hold. It'll never happen. Not without a bit of magic and the right bolts anyway."

"Is that so?" Aunt Thelma said with raised eyebrows.

"I'll make sure to let him know." I excused myself to talk with Benny and give the two women a chance to catch up in private. I'd bet any money Benny hadn't used the right bolts or any magic, and I wanted to prevent another mishap if at all possible.

"If you'd like any help, I'd love to lend a hand. We could even film it!" Sophia hollered after me.

I turned around.

Aunt Thelma's eyes brightened.

Sophia rubbed her fingers together absentmind-edly, making the symbol for cash, as she re-designed the space in her head.

"I think we're going to pass," I replied, cautiously.

"What? Why. I think it's a great idea," Aunt Thelma scoffed.

"I don't know. We don't have a lot of time, and the last thing we need is more people here. It's chaotic enough." I jumped back as Percy flew in front of my face, my foot slipping on the tile floor as I tried to get out of his way. Thankfully I caught my balance.

"Wouldn't it be great for advertising?" Aunt Thelma drew the last word out, emphasizing it. "You're the one that's always on my case about drumming up business."

"It would be if had planned it out right, which we didn't. Maybe next time?"

I could see Aunt Thelma wanted to continue the discussion, but now wasn't the right time, not in front of Sophia.

"Can we talk about this later? I want to tell Benny about the bolt." I turned back around before my aunt could reply.

"Oh, don't listen to Angelica. She has her wand in a knot with this renovation. We'll convince her tonight," Aunt Thelma conspired behind me, not bothering to hide it.

I closed my eyes, and took a calming breath. Later, in private, I'd explain to my aunt why I thought Sophia's suggestion was a bad idea. You didn't just open your business to a production crew on a whim. Given the way the inn looked, they'd paint us as the most incompetent witches who ever lived this side of Salem —and broadcast it. I shivered, mortified at the thought.

When I opened my eyes, I had the contractor in my sights. Right, the bolt. Shoulders set square, and atti-tude readjusted, I headed his way.

I made it two steps when something fell from the ceiling, just missing my head. Instinctively, I jumped back. This time I wasn't so lucky. My hands flew out to protect myself, but the tile slipped from under my feet, causing me to fall on my backside. Glass shattered in front of me at the same time.

"What the devil?" Sophia replied.

I looked above at the recessed light socket where a bulb once hung.

Aunt Thelma rushed to give me a hand up. "You okay, dear?"

I winced. That was going to leave a bruise on my backside, but other than that, I was fine.

"And you thought I was trouble," Percy sailed through the lobby with a chuckle. He was right. I'd take a trickster ghost any day to this mess.

"Who didn't screw in the lightbulbs?" Benny yelled from the ladder.

"I can see you guys are very busy here. How about I run into town, say my hellos, and pop back in a couple of hours?" Sophia backtracked out of her offer to help and out of the inn as her feet inched backward.

"That would be perfect!" Aunt Thelma beamed as if everything would be right as rain by then. I wasn't so sure.

"I'll see you soon!" Sophia disappeared out the door as fast as her heels could safely carry her.

"What are we going to do?" I groaned once Sophia was safely out of earshot.

"Don't panic. I have everything under control."

I gave my aunt the side-eye. Her idea of under control was vastly different from mine. "Don't give me that look. It's not attractive. Now first thing's first, we need to miniaturize those boxes. That way, we can move them in a snap." Aunt Thelma snapped her fingers for emphasis. "Then I'll activate some charms and voilà. Easy, peasy, lemon squeezy!"

"I think it's stressy, depressy, lemon zesty," I sighed, having a bad feeling about all of this.

Aunt Thelma chose to ignore me. "Now, where is my wand?"

"Did you check the cookie jar?"

"It's not in the cookie jar." Aunt Thelma dismissed my comment as absurd.

"It could be." On more than one occasion, I'd found my aunt's wand in odd places like the refrigerator, her tea pot, and even the microwave.

"On second thought, you might be right. And if not, I can snag a cookie while I look. Have you tried Diane's double chocolate ones? They're to die for."

Diane was the owner of La Luna Bakery, and her desserts were heavenly. For the first time that morning, I found myself agreeing with my aunt.

CHAPTER TWO

I had to admit, miniaturizing the boxes had been a brilliant idea. It only took two grocery bags full to carry the now three by three-inch square boxes that were once ten times as big to my room. I dropped the bags on my bed and caught my reflection in the mirror. Stress lines creased my forehead and dark circles bruised under my eyes. Aunt Thelma was right, it was not an attractive look. I used my fingertips and attempted to smooth the creases away and promised myself I'd turn in early that night.

My phone chimed in my pocket, snapping me out of my self-assessment.

"Where are you?" The message read. It was from Diane, who was also one of the festival committee members.

"Gah! The festival meeting!" I'd completely forgotten. So much for relaxing. The stress lines were instantly back in place. I turned on my heel and jogged downstairs to where Aunt Thelma was bibity bobity booing the guest rooms.

"What spell would fix this?" Aunt Thelma asked herself as she stared at the oversized floral wallpaper. Her wand was in one hand and a cookie in the other.

"Aunt Thelma—"

"Your meeting. Yes, I just remembered. You go. Don't worry. I have everything under control."

"You sure?"

"Honey, please." Aunt Thelma gave me a pointed look.

"Good point." Where spells were concerned, she was the more skilled witch. I gave her arm a squeeze as I passed through.

Normally, I'd take the Enchanted Trail over to Village Square for my meeting—the quaint shopping district was a fifteen-minute walk along the lake—but today, I didn't have time.

I snagged Aunt Thelma's car keys from the office, yelled over the workmen that I was borrowing her car, and headed out the door. The sounds of nature outside were a welcome respite, and the change in decibels was profound. I thought my ears were ringing from the buzz saw for a second, but it turned out to be a symphony of insects as they joined in the chorus. I preferred nature's soundtrack any day to calamity inside Mystic Inn. I decided then and there that it was good to get out, if only for a quick meeting.

It was a short drive around the bend and over the stream to Village Square's parking lot. Sidewalks and flagstone paths connected the storybook shops. If you were lucky, you found a parking spot up front along the perimeter. If not, you had to park in one of the side lots and make your way over to the shops on foot.

Today, I was not lucky, and at this point, I wasn't surprised. As I circled the parking lot, looking for a place to park, I glanced over at Wishing Well Park to see how the festival's setup was going. With its ample, green space and towering fountain, the park was a perfect spot to host the festival. Local business owners had all pitched in to make the event happen, including donating money for the stage Mr. McCormick, town council member, and greenhouse manager, was currently assembling. Vendors were at various stages of setting up their booths. Red and white striped tents dotted the landscape. Once word got out about the festival, witches from all over the region flocked to Silverlake to sign up. Adding vendors turned out to be a smart idea as it brought in additional revenue, which the town desperately needed. That was, after all, what inspired me to suggest the festival in the first place.

I waved at Connie, owner of the potions shop, Mix it Up!, as she pushed a dolly stacked with clear totes full of glass vials. Shimmery blue, sparkling green, and vibrant red liquid shown through the transparent containers. I assumed she was headed to the park to set up shop. It had been Connie's idea to create a local marketplace featuring samples of the Village Square shops in the park. The idea was people would like what they saw and head over to the shopping district to buy more. Then, out-of-town vendors contacted us and asked if they could come too, and the town council said yes (well, the majority of them anyway.) Now here we were with a packed park just waiting for tourists to arrive.

When all was said and done, it took me just as long to find a spot to park and walk over to the cafe as it would have if I'd just hoofed it down the Enchanted Trail. Lesson learned.

"Sorry, I'm late!" I walked into the cafe and joined the festival committee's table. The professional in me loathed being late. As if on cue, Heather, my one-time future mother-in-law-to-be and cafe owner, dropped by with a tall glass and a pitcher of peach iced tea.

"Don't worry. We haven't even started yet," Diane said.

"Only ordered lunch," Roger added. Roger was Diane's significant other and owner of the flower shop.

"The usual?" Heather asked me as she filled my glass.

"I suppose I could eat." It was pointless to resist Heather's Monte Cristo. I didn't know her secret, but somehow the combination of the fried bread, melted cheese, and honey ham sandwich topped with powdered sugar and served with homemade raspberry preserves spoke to my soul—and my waistline. I had indulged in the buttery fried goodness one too many times lately. I would have to make time for exercise, something I had been religious about in Chicago. If I could run on a boring treadmill in my apartment, I could certainly hit the Enchanted Trail now and then. I needed to get back into it for both my physical health and mental health.

"How's the inn coming?" Clemmie asked. Clemmie was my aunt's best friend and another member of the committee. She owned the local tea shop, and together she and my aunt were trouble.

"Don't ask," I replied, taking a long sip of my drink. "Sophia Emerson just checked in."

"That's horrible luck," Roger said.

I nodded at him. "You can say that again."

"Never did like her. She's totally phony," Clemmie confessed.

"I agree," Diane added.

"Don't let Aunt Thelma hear you say that." I punched my straw through the wrapper as I spoke. "She's never uttered a bad word about her. Aunt Thelma admires her too darn much.

"Thelma's been under that woman's spell for years," Clemmie said with a head shake. "Ever since high school. I, for one, was pleased as punch when she moved away, but Thelma moped for days. You think I'm kidding, but I'm not. I was convinced Sophia spelled her a time or two."

"I don't doubt it. When Sophia stole my pumpkin pie recipe, Thelma wouldn't listen to me. She said it must've been a coincidence, but the recipe was word for word. Secret ingredient and all!" Diane got hot just thinking about it.

"She stole your recipe?" I asked.

"Page six of Kitchen Witch, Volume 1." Diane tapped her fingernail on the table.

"That's awful. I'm so sorry." I couldn't believe Sophia could be so callous.

"It's not your fault, but speaking of apologies, I never did get one," Diane grumbled.

Clemmie changed the subject, "Tell Thelma I'll be there in two shakes of a broom tail tonight after I close up shop. Heaven knows Sophia isn't going to do a thing to help."

I debated telling the group about Sophia's offer to film a segment at the inn but decided not to. Our conversation was already off-track, and the meeting delayed. With busy lives and businesses to manage, I figured we should get to work. But I did tell Clemmie that she might want to rethink that offer seeing Sophia and Arthur were due for dinner.

"Well, tell her to call me regardless. I'll drop by if she needs me," Clemmie insisted.

"Will do," I replied.

But getting down to business was easier said than done.

Clemmie and Diane were still complaining about Sophia when my ex, Vance, walked into the cafe. He stopped next to his mother, planted a kiss on her cheek, waved hello to the rest of us, and sat at the lunch counter to put in an order.

"You're blushing," my friend Misty said as she walked in and joined our table. It appeared that I wasn't the only one running late.

"Am not," I shot back like a child even though I could feel the heat spread across my face. Vance and I had history with a capital H, but I was determined to remain in the here and now. We were friends. Nothing more. Nothing less. And that's the way it was going to stay.

"Now that we're all here, should we get started then?" Diane asked.

"Yes, let's. How are we with the permits? Roger everything signed, sealed, and official?" I asked.

"Sure is, but Mayor Crabby Patty isn't too happy about it," Roger said dryly.

"Mayor Parrish can stuff it. She and the rest of the council haven't done a darn thing in years to help us," Clemmie said.

"Preach," Misty replied, grabbing a sesame stick from the center of the table and snapping it in two.

"Speak of the devil," Diane said, looking over her shoulder. I turned in time to see Mayor Parrish walk into the cafe. She wore a navy-blue business dress with coordinating pumps and enough gold accessories to shine like a beacon. She was lucky she was walking the streets of Silverlake and not strutting her stuff in Chicago. A robber wouldn't be able to pass her up.

"Well, if it isn't the bucket brigade. What hodge-podge idea are you cooking up today? Adding pig races to your hoedown?" Mayor Parrish snorted at her joke.

"That's not a bad idea," Roger quipped.

"Don't you dare. That's just the sort of thing Harrisville would do." Mayor Parrish scoffed, referencing a nearby town whose tourism hadn't suffered like ours had. Even though the town wasn't enchanted, the mayor was a witch, and he knew how to work his magic. "You might've gotten the council to agree to this little festival of yours, but I'm still the mayor." Mayor Parrish jabbed a finger at her chest.

"How could we ever forget?" Misty's voice was a little too sweet. She and Mayor Parrish stared hard at one another. Neither one of them backing down.

"Your latte, Madame Mayor," Heather interrupted, handing over the clear, plastic to-go cup. I could tell Heather was in a hurry to see the mayor walk out of the cafe.

"Oh, why, thank you," Mayor Parrish took the latte from Heather's hand. "I trust it's the way I like it?"

"Grande, iced, sugar-free, vanilla latte with almond milk," Heather replied in one breath.

"That'll do." Mayor Parrish turned around with a rather smug expression on her face.

"That woman's a pill," I said as the mayor walked out the door.

"She's something else, too," Clemmie replied.

"Honestly, you would think she'd be happy we came up with a plan to save the town," Diane remarked.

"Oh, she would be if it had been her idea," Roger said.

"And if the idea was more upscale," Diane added. It was no secret Mayor Parrish enjoyed the finer things in life.

By the end of the meeting, our task lists had grown

considerably. Roger needed to call back last-minute vendors and tell them we could fit them in and get their paperwork signed.

Diane was overseeing the pie competition. Bakers could enter any fall favorite, and the applications were rolling in. I had lined up Diane, Sophia, and Mayor Parrish as the judges, hoping it would change the mayor's attitude, but clearly, I'd been mistaken.

Clemmie and Misty were the official welcome wagon — signing in vendors, making sure they were set up in the right spot, and answering any of their questions.

Roger nicknamed me the fire chief. Not that Silverlake didn't already have a fire chief. No, my job was to run around and put out the festival's proverbial fires, like finding a replacement tractor for the hayrides after Mr. McCormick's took a dive. I also needed to find replacement face painters after the cheerleading pyramid collapsed and more than one squad member was nursing a sore wrist.

"I think we need to meet someplace else tomorrow." I sat back from the table, my pants feeling uncomfortably tight.

"Fine by me," Misty replied, looking as slim as ever. Come to think of it, my best friend's muscle tone looked impressive. The girl must be working out.

"How about my shop? I've been fiddling with this new pumpkin spice blend for too long. I need somebody else's opinion." Clemmie shook her head like she couldn't believe tea could give her so much trouble. Knowing Clemmie, the brew was perfect.

"Same time?" Roger asked over the rim of his bifocals. He didn't wear them all the time, only when needed, like now while examining the bill.

"I'm good with that if you all are." I looked around the table. Diane, Misty, and Clemmie agreed. "Okay, guys, until tomorrow then."

CHAPTER THREE

With the meeting adjourned and lunch over, we got ready to leave. Our chairs scraped across the hardwood floor as we stood from the table. Diane bent forward, picking up our silverware and stacking the plates to make the busboy's job easier and give Heather a hand. I followed suit with our straw wrappers and used napkins. The lunch rush was in full effect, and Heather could use an extra set of hands.

"Thank you!" She hollered from behind the lunch counter as we exited the cafe.

"You doing okay? You look rough." Leave it to Misty to tell me like it was. She had waited until we were the only two standing outside together.

I waved one final goodbye to Diane as she and Roger walked away from us down the sidewalk toward his flower shop.

I turned back to Misty. She searched my face for an answer. "What's wrong?"

"It's nothing."

"And my middle name's not Merryweather."

"Your middle name's Merryweather?"

"After my godmother. You knew that. My point is, you're stressed. I can see it. What's wrong?"

"Same thing that's been wrong all week. The inn's trashed, and I honestly don't think it'll be ready by Friday."

"It can't be that bad." Misty tried to dismiss my concerns, but she hadn't seen the place. Not since we demoed it weeks ago.

I gave my friend a pointed look. "The whole point of the festival was to drum up business and put Silverlake back on the map, but now all that's at stake. I shouldn't have agreed to my aunt's timeline. It was too soon."

"If I recall, you didn't have much of a choice."

I remembered that fateful meeting not too long ago, when not only had the town agreed to host a festival, but Lyle Peters wound up dead. A chill ran down my spine.

Misty was right, though. The business owners hadn't wanted to wait. They needed the tourists to return, and quickly.

"I know. You're right, but still."

"You feel responsible."

"I do." Both the festival and renovation were my ideas. The timeline, however, was not.

"What does Thelma say?"

"You know how she is. Everything's fine! It's going

to be great." I raised the pitch of my voice, doing my best Thelma Nightingale impersonation.

"Maybe she's right."

"Or maybe she's not. You're talking about the woman who let the inn fall into disrepair in the first place."

"Good point. What are you going to do?"

"I'm not sure. I'm on my ninth contingency plan." If I were at my old job, I never would've agreed to such an extensive renovation before a big event. I was more annoyed at myself than anything else for letting Aunt Thelma talk me into it. She might be the inn's owner, but she looked to me to manage it. I knew better.

"You know what you need?" Misty asked.

"A new contractor?" I replied hopefully.

"Probably, but that's not what I was going to say."

"You better not say a date."

"Also true, but no. Did I tell you Peter asked me out?"

"He did? Good for you." Peter was the wand shop owner, Sticks, and Misty had been eying him from afar.

"Yep, he beat me to it. I caught up to him on the trail yesterday. He asked me to go to the festival with him." Misty bit her bottom lip, pleased with herself.

"Are you blushing?" I joked, giving Misty a hard time.

Misty swatted my arm. "No. But it's nice to know he's into me. Anyway, that's not what I was going to say. I was going to say you need to go for a run with me."

I let out a breath. Now that I could agree to. Hadn't

I been thinking I needed to work out? And wasn't I also saying how good Misty looked? "I was going to tell you that you look good. I noticed at lunch."

"Oh yeah?" Misty turned to the side. Fists on her hips, shoulders pulled back, she jokingly showed off her svelte form.

"You're ridiculous."

"I know. That's why you love me. Now, what do you say? Meet me here tomorrow at eight?" We were now standing in front of the bookstore. "We can hit the Enchanted Trail."

"Sounds like a plan. I'll see you tomorrow."

"It's a date." Misty turned to head into the bookstore. "See you later," she called over her shoulder.

I was going to say goodbye, but then I had an idea. "Hey, wait. Do you sell any home-improvement books?"

"Of course. I think I have all of Sophia's."

"Oh, the irony." I shook my head. As much as I wanted to do the renovation the good, old-fashioned way, I wasn't naive and knew we needed magic on our side. I just didn't know where to start.

"Come on in." Misty held the door for me.

Now and then, there's a place that resonates with you. A place that makes you smile the moment you enter, no matter how you felt two seconds before. That's what Spellbinding Books was to me. Aunt Thelma used to bring me here when I was a kid on Saturday mornings for cookies and storytime, and now it's where I came on Saturday mornings with a latte in hand and to catch up with Misty.

The bookstore was shaped like a piece of pie—narrow in the front and curved wide in the back—and you could bet I had a favorite reading nook. It was the chair right under one of the factory-sized windows that flanked the back door. If I didn't have so much to do, I'd grab a book and curl up there right this minute. *Maybe next weekend*, I thought wistfully.

"You want Connie to set up upstairs, right?" Vicki Love, Misty's coworker, asked my friend when we walked in.

Connie, the potions shop owner, stood next to Vicki. Her wares stacked beside her.

It turned out I had been wrong. Connie wasn't setting up shop at the park. She was setting up shop here.

"Yes. I'll help in a minute. Let me show Angelica something first." Misty turned on her heel, and I followed her to the back of the store. "Connie's doing a potion demo this afternoon. A practice one before her big book release this weekend."

"Good idea." Connie wrote a potions book that she'd planned to release on Halloween but bumped up the date to coincide with the festival. I'd previously flipped through the book, and my skills paled in comparison. Connie's potions could make you sleep like a baby (or the dead if you overdid it), have someone fall madly in love with you, restore your youth—or tackle more domestic tasks like removing baked-on grease from your oven and stubborn laundry stains.

Sophia Emerson better watch out. Connie could be the next big witch on the scene.

Truth be told, potions had never been my strong suit. If anything, transformation work had. I absent-mindedly reached for the tiger's eye pendant around my neck. The necklace offered more than protection. It allowed me, and only me, the power to transform into a cat. A gift passed down through the first-born females on my mother's side. But other than that, I was still woefully ignorant. Connie said she planned on performing a demo each day of the event. It was a win-win all around. The demos should drive people into the store, which would increase sales for Misty, get Connie more exposure, and perhaps I could learn a thing or two.

Misty led me to the store's back left corner but stopped abruptly. I had to put my hand on her shoulder to brace myself because she stopped so fast.

The sound of two people arguing reached my ears.

"You're a fake, and we all know it. Unless you want me to tell the rest of the world, you know what you need to do." I held onto Misty's shoulder. Together we peered around the bookshelf. A tall man with broad shoulders and dark hair curled around the nape of his neck towered over Sophia. His t-shirt was stained with streaks of a tar-like substance, matching his worn-through jeans and steel-toe work boots.

Sophia stood straight. Shoulders back, hands on her hips, her expression twisted in disdain.

"You've got some nerve." Her voice seemed amused.

It was unnaturally sweet, as if she smiled while delivering the line, and the man had no idea who she was or what she was capable of.

The man chuckled darkly. "I've got more than nerve. And you've been warned."

Sophia's eyes narrowed, but she held her tongue.

Misty and I were still standing there when the man turned away, shooting a parting glare over his shoulder before walking out the bookstore's back entrance.

Sophia's carefully controlled expression slid back into place like a deadbolt. She turned back to the bookshelf and began perusing the titles. Her finger traced along the volumes' spines.

Misty and I backtracked to the counter.

"Who was that?" I kept my voice low as if we were in a library and not a bookstore. I knew most of the long-term residents, but not everyone. A lot of people came and left Silverlake in the thirteen years I lived in Chicago.

"Rick Kelly."

"How does he know Sophia?"

"I'm not sure." Misty raised her eyebrow in thought.

"They don't look like they'd run in the same circle." Sophia's designer business attire sprung to mind at my words.

"Or the same universe."

"Exactly." I thought for a minute before adding, "One thing's for certain."

"What's that?"

"Looks like Diane and Clemmie aren't the only

ones who know Sophia's secret." I filled Misty in on what they'd said at lunch before she got there.

"Sophia, find something you like?" Misty's voice was louder than necessary, signaling for me to shut my mouth.

"I do like your selection," Sophia said with a smirk, holding her book in hand. "I thought I might sign a couple and put them back on the shelf. Would that be all right with you?"

"Absolutely. Let me get you a pen." Misty reached below the counter.

"Oh no, I always carry my own," Sophia removed the black-capped marker from her leather handbag and held it up for us to see. "It's important to always be prepared. Fans are everywhere," Sophia smiled, but it didn't quite reach her eyes.

Misty and I smiled politely in return before I eyed my friend knowingly. Silverlake's most famous resident couldn't get back to California fast enough.

CHAPTER FOUR

I made it back to the inn after finding a working tractor to pull the kids around for hayrides and stopping by the high school to recruit a new batch of face painters.

The day felt much later than the hour would have me believe. The fact that the sun was setting earlier and earlier wasn't helping either. The golden rays of the midday sun had given way to streaks of red and orange as the sun sank closer to the horizon.

"At least something is going right," I said as I spotted the carpet delivery van. From the looks of it, they brought the right carpet this time versus the red plaid atrocity they tried to install last week.

The words were barely out of my mouth when the installer, Henry, walked over to my car. I opened the door and stepped out. "Hi, Henry. Glad you made it back in time."

"About that." Henry looked down at his feet.

Oh no. I knew it wasn't going to be good.

"I'm real sorry, Ms. Angelica, but it looks like they shorted us some."

"How much is some?" I winced. I was almost too afraid to ask.

The man calculated the total in his head, "Oh, I'd say about three thousand square feet?"

In other words, the entire second floor. I groaned and stared up at the sky, hoping the answer would rain down upon me. "How soon can we get it?"

"I don't know. Guess I can make some calls and find out."

I sighed for what must have been the tenth time since my day had begun. Henry took a step back, probably afraid I was going to yell at him. But I wouldn't do that. Even frustrated, I knew Henry wasn't to blame. I would, however, like to see the order form Benny submitted. My faith in the contractor was dwindling by the day.

"Okay, will you let me know what you find out? I'll just be inside."

"Will do, ma'am." Henry got right on his phone while I bent back down and gathered my things out of the car. From the sound of the conversation, it didn't sound like we'd have our carpet anytime soon. My aunt knew a lot of spells, but I wasn't sure what she could do about the carpet. I guess there only was one way to find out.

"They don't have enough carpet," I said to Aunt Thelma when I walked in the door.

She was standing behind the check-in counter. Her red hair pulled back in a messy bun. A pencil pinched between her lips. Her planner sat open on the countertop.

"I'm sure they can get more," she said, taking the pencil from her mouth.

"I know, but will it get here in time?" I knew the answer was most likely not.

"We could jazz it up a bit." Aunt Thelma did jazz hands for emphasis.

"And by jazz, you mean use a spell to make it look like the rest?" In my mind, I replayed the scene in Sleeping Beauty where the fairy godmothers fought over changing Arora's dress from blue to pink. I didn't think Aunt Thelma would get carried away like Flora and Merryweather. But then again, she did just use jazz hands.

"Or I suppose I could do that." Aunt Thelma looked down at her planner. "Wouldn't be as much fun," she muttered.

"Let me tell Henry to install whatever decent carpet they can find."

"Good idea," Aunt Thelma agreed.

I walked back out and relayed the plan to Henry. In a perfect world, the carpeting would all match without magic. But this wasn't the perfect world, and now wasn't the time for perfection. A fact that was hard for me to admit. It was crunch time.

"Sophia come back?" I asked once back inside.

Aunt Thelma answered by motioning out the glass

doors toward the lake. Sophia and her husband Arthur were taking a romantic canoe ride for two. Arthur paddled the boat ashore while Sophia drank a glass of wine. Sophia leaned forward, causing Arthur to quit paddling for a moment. Just long enough for her to meet him halfway with a kiss.

Aunt Thelma shook her head longingly. "Now there's a marriage done right."

Arthur laughed about something. Sophia blushed and swatted his leg playfully.

I had to agree with my aunt. The couple did look like the picture of happiness even through my jaded eyes. Their body language alone revealed how happy and comfortable they were with one another.

"How long have they been together?" I asked.

"Oh, since high school. Two peas in a pod, those two. They're lucky to have found love so young." There was a hint of sadness in my aunt's voice. I reached out and patted her hand. Aunt Thelma had never been lucky in love. In fact, she was rather unlucky. Hopefully, that would change in the future.

"Enough with the ho-hums. Let's get that dinner order called in, shall we?" Aunt Thelma grabbed the cordless phone off the counter and walked outside to greet her friends and get their orders.

"Happy sappy couple," Percy appeared beside me, singing the words and then pretending to vomit.

"Aw, somebody needs a girlfriend," I replied.

"I do not! Girl ghosts are gross."

"Uh-huh. Who could we set you up with?" I

pretended to ponder my paranormal choices. "Isn't there a nice banshee haunting the tavern? I heard her shackles are pretty cute."

"They are not!"

Percy's defensiveness peaked my interest.

"Are you blushing? Is Percy the Poltergeist embarrassed?"

"I'm not blushing, and Melinda's shackles aren't cute!"

"So, she has a name. I'll have to keep that in mind."

POOF!

Percy disappeared with a flash.

I had only been joking, but it turned out I might have been on to something. You could bet I was going to keep Percy's crush in my back pocket. It might save me from having to call him Your Majesty like I had to all last month for doing me a favor.

I ended up ordering the lemon chicken pasta instead of the famous filet or ribeye dinner the Simmering Spoon was known for. I felt like a dose of carbs and butter was just what the doctor ordered, even if I might regret come tomorrow morning's run.

Aunt Thelma had been right about one thing, eating dinner on the patio had been a great idea. If I didn't look through the glass lobby windows, I could almost forget how torn up everything was inside. And if I could have ignored the sound of Sophia's constantly ringing cell phone, I might have even been able to relax. The weather was perfect. It was one of those beautiful autumn evenings where the southern heat sunk with the sun and almost made you reach for a sweater. I was still used to Chicago weather. In Illinois, we'd be bundled up in sweatshirts and jeans by now. Maybe even hats and mittens, depending on which way the wind blew off the lake. In the wintertime, the wind got so blistering cold my eyes would water just stepping outside.

"How's Mike doing?" Aunt Thelma asked as she cut into her ribeye.

"What's that?" Arthur didn't seem to have a clue as to what Aunt Thelma was talking about.

"Didn't you go golfing with Mike McCormick today?" Aunt Thelma questioned. Sophia was chewing and stared at her husband. She gave a slight nod for confirmation.

"Oh, right. Yes, Mike's great. Lousy at the tee box as ever." Arthur chuckled. It was an empty sound and had my witchy instincts twitching.

"You two always have had a friendly rivalry, haven't you?" Sophia said after swallowing and taking a drink of her wine. She reached beside her and lovingly squeezed the top of her husband's hand resting on the table.

Sophia had changed for dinner, embracing Silverlake's true outdoor nature with a pale turquoise, down vest, a long-sleeved, white t-shirt, khaki pants, and hiking boots. It was as if she had stepped off the pages of a Lands' End catalogue and onto our patio.

Arthur replied with another smile that didn't meet his eyes. If you read between the lines, you knew there was history there. I guess you could say, when it came to small towns, you couldn't throw a stone without hitting drama. It came with the territory.

Sophia's phone rang for the third time. She glanced at the screen and quickly silenced it like she had the other times. I had no idea how the woman ever found any peace. Hopefully, the phone hadn't rung the entire time she was out on the lake with Arthur. I had lived the nonstop notification life for long enough and knew how exhausting it could be. Another benefit to moving back home — the slower lifestyle. Not that it was sleepy or stress-free. No, sometimes it felt like I traded out one type of stress for another. But even with everything happening at the inn, there was no question about it— I was happier living in Silverlake. Happier now that I could admit that I was a witch (even if I wasn't a very good one.) I was still annoyed with myself for running away from who I was for the last decade, but I also knew that I couldn't change the past and that everything happened for a reason. I guess I should be grateful that I remembered who I was before having a life full of regret.

It hadn't been two minutes from the last time Sophia's phone rang when it was going off again.

"I guess I better take this. Excuse me." Sophia got up from the table and hurried off inside the lobby.

Arthur followed his wife with his eyes. His expression guarded. An underlying emotion hid below the surface. It was there in his eyes. He looked frustrated or perhaps disappointed. It was hard to say.

"'That phone never stops ringing," Arthur kept his voice low.

"Maybe soon though, huh?" Aunt Thelma was ever the optimist. Turning to me, she said, "Sophia told me she's thinking of retiring."

"Oh? That sounds promising." To help silence the calls, that is.

"I'll believe it when I see it," Arthur replied over the rim of his glasses, unable to keep the sadness out of his voice.

I went to reach for my wine glass when I noticed it was almost empty. As was Arthur's, and Aunt Thelma's would be soon. Unfortunately, so was the bottle. Not judging, but Sophia could down the chardonnay. Being the ever-gracious host, I excused myself, walked through the inn's lobby, ignored Sophia on the phone, and headed for the small downstairs kitchen. Aunt Thelma had a wine fridge that she kept fully stocked in the inn's kitchenette. Guests could buy the wine by the glass or bottle, same with champagne. Unfortunately for Sophia, that had been our last bottle of chardonnay. I eyed the remaining bottles, trying to decide which one would be the next best choice. Perhaps a pinot grigio or maybe sauvignon blanc? Both of those were fairly dry white wines, similar to chardonnay. I thought about asking Sophia, who I could still hear talking on the phone, which one she preferred. I was sure she'd have a preference on the matter.

I poked my head out of the kitchen and looked to where Sophia was talking.

Perhaps she didn't realize it, or maybe she didn't even care, but the empty lobby made everything echo, including her voice.

"I told you, I needed space... don't threaten me. You need to back off. You don't own me." Sophia's voice was like steel — cold and hard. Her words had me tiptoeing back into the kitchen, where I decided to grab both a bottle of pinot grigio and sauvignon blanc, knowing that I could even come back for the reisling if it turned out that's what she preferred.

"Everything alright?" Aunt Thelma asked when I rejoined her and Arthur at the table.

She must've read the apprehension on my face. Sophia's words repeated in my head and I wondered if it was Rick Kelly on the other end of the line. Whatever beef he had with Sophia, he wasn't backing down. Their conversations piqued both my curiosity and concern.

I wiped my expression clean.

"Yes. I wasn't sure which one you'd all prefer, so I brought a selection." I held the two bottles up in the air for emphasis.

I wasn't sure if my aunt bought my explanation, but she dropped the subject.

Sophia rejoined our group as I opened the sauvignon blanc (Arthur's choice).

"It really is lovely out here." She gazed across the lake.

That wasn't what I'd thought Sophia was going to say. But then again, she might not want everyone knowing her business. Make that she probably didn't want *me* to know. I was pretty sure she'd tell Arthur and Aunt Thelma what had happened today. With that thought, I decided I would excuse myself after dinner and give the trio a chance to catch up.

"I've always been jealous of you, Thelma. You have your own piece of paradise right here." Sophia smiled. If I hadn't overheard the conversation, I would have never suspected anything was amiss. I suppose that was just the way it was in show business. Yet again, another reason why I was happy with who I was and where I was living.

CHAPTER FIVE

The following day, I was happy that I hadn't overindulged in the pasta. The idea of waking up early to go for a run always sounds better in theory than in practice. But I was disciplined, or I tried to remind myself that I had been at one time, and I knew it was always hardest to start something. If I were serious about exercise, it would only be harder to start tomorrow. The one good thing about not working out for a while was that I had my choice of what to wear. No excuses there. As I laced up my running shoes, I'm not going to lie, I debated driving to Spellbinding Books to meet Misty. Realizing that was ridiculous, I bypassed Aunt Thelma's keys and headed out through the front entrance.

Surprisingly, Percy, who gladly took the midnight shift at the inn, kept his smart mouth to himself. Nothing about me needing exercise or asking about cobwebs in my running shoes—both of which wouldn't have surprised me. Something must be on the poltergeist's mind. I wondered if it was Melinda.

Even though I was a bit sleepy, I would rather run in the morning than later in the day. Evenings might be cooling off, but midday could still be brutal in the full southern sun. Not only that, but I wanted to get it out of the way and start my day on a positive note. I was serious when I said I needed to calm down and relax. Exercising was one way to do that, or so the experts said.

I walked around the front of the inn as opposed to going out the lobby's back doors. The patio might be lovely, but the beach surrounded it, and I hated getting sand in my shoes. It would be impossible to get out, and then it would be between my toes. I shuddered.

After a couple of quick stretches and deep breaths at the trailhead, I set off down the path at a brisk pace. I had to admit that it felt good being up and moving. Birds were chirping, swans glided across the lake, and even the mosquitoes seemed to have better things to do than trail after me. I could get used to this. It sure beat hitting the treadmill or running outside in the frigid midwestern winters.

Thinking about Chicago pulled me back into the past. I couldn't think about my old life without appreciating where I was now, both mentally and physically. I had my family and friends to thank for that—especially Aunt Thelma and her trickster ways. She knew me better than I knew myself, even though she hadn't laid eyes on me in months. I had a smile on my face from the gratitude I felt in my heart, and I didn't have a care in the world. I hated to sound cliche, but I truly felt blessed. For the first time in a long time, I knew I was where I belonged.

I was happy and content.

And the morning was off to a perfect start.

That is until a shocking sight hit my eyes.

At first, it looked like a lifejacket bobbing in the water, but I quickly realized there was a body attached to it. It wasn't a lifejacket but a puffy, down vest. The same vest Sophia wore last night.

Without even thinking, I ran into the water. My feet sunk into the muck as I trudged forward. The water quickly became waist-deep. I gave up walking and swam forward. Sophia's body was about thirty feet from shore. Her upper body was prone, with her face below the water. Even with the water buoyancy's added help, I struggled to get my arm around Sophia and turn her over. In my mind, I knew it was too late. One look at her, and I knew that she had drowned some time ago, but that didn't stop me from trying my hardest to save her. I needed to get her ashore quickly. With one arm around her waist, I labored forward. As soon as my feet touched the bottom, I put both of my arms under Sophia's armpits and walked backward. Once again, my feet sank into the muck. The lake bottom captured my shoe, pulling it off in the process.

"Help! I need help!" My voice echoed off the lake. "HELP!" I yelled even louder. I lifted Sophia on the bank as much as possible. Her legs were still in the water, but her water-logged torso was on dry land.

"Angelica?" Misty yelled back my name.

"Over here!" I stood, panting, soaked to the bone with only one shoe on. I looked down at Sophia. There was no point in administering CPR or attempting magic. There wasn't any spell that could bring some-body back from the grave.

Misty ran to meet me. "Are you okay? What's going —" Misty caught sight of Sophia's body and quickly put two and two together. "Oh my gosh. She's dead," Misty's voice was full of shock.

"I know." I hunched over, hands on my thighs, as I still fought to control my breath. "Do you have your cell phone on you?" Mine was soaked in my pocket.

Misty took her phone out and called the sheriff's department.

"Hey, it's Misty. There's been an accident," she said when the lines connected. "It's Sophia Emerson. We just found her in the lake. She drowned."

There were some questions on the other end of the line.

"We're on the Enchanted Trail, between Mystic Inn and the tavern. Yes, us being Angelica Nightingale and me."

I had to hand it to Misty. She sounded calmer than I could've ever been. With her hand on her hip and her head held high, she was cool, calm, and in charge.

Misty hung up the phone. "They're on their way. You okay?"

"Yeah, I think so." I shook my head in disbelief. "Poor Arthur and Aunt Thelma." I looked away from Sophia. There were some things a person never wanted to see, and this was one of them. I gave Misty my full attention. "I'm thankful you heard me."

"Me too. I was walking down the trail, planning on meeting you halfway."

I nodded. In the distance, we heard sirens heading our way.

People always say time moves slowly when you're waiting for help, and that morning, it was no exception. I felt powerless to help Sophia or do anything to right the situation.

That feeling quickly dissipated when the sheriff's deputies arrived on the scene.

They say you shouldn't hate anyone, but there are some people who you really, really don't like, and one of them was walking towards me right now. I despised Amber Reynolds when we were in high school, and that feeling had only grown since she had become a deputy. A deputy with an equal feeling of animosity for me.

Thankfully, Deputy Jones was also with her. I turned his way, ready to ignore Deputy Reynolds and give the younger man my attention. But of course, Amber wasn't about to pass up the opportunity to harass me.

"I'm not surprised. A dead body's called in, and you're at the scene." Amber smirked.

I folded my arms defensively across my chest. My arms felt like ice below my elbows.

"How about, thanks for calling this in. Are you okay?" Misty schooled Deputy Reynolds on her job.

"*Are* you okay?" Deputy Jones asked me.

"I am. But Sophia's not."

Deputy Jones walked over and began examining the body.

"You pulled her in?" he asked me.

I nodded. "She was about thirty feet out. Facedown in the water."

"A regular hero," Amber replied sarcastically.

We all chose to ignore Amber. Besides, at that time, our quartet grew as the medical examiner arrived. Dr. Fitz Humphrey looked like the werewolf he could shift into with his thick silver fur—I mean hair—and his short, clipped beard. Medical examiner was just one of the many hats the man wore, as he was one of the only two private practice doctors in Silverlake. The other one was Constance, a witch who incorporated more spells and potions into her practice than traditional medicine. Constance and Dr. Fitz complemented one another in their skill sets. For example, Constance would've never been able to pluck Sophia out of the water as if she were a paper doll the way Dr. Fitz did with his animalistic strength.

Amber was forced to quit harassing me and join her colleagues while Dr. Fitz began his lakeside examination.

"What do you think happened?" Misty asked in

hush tones.

"I have no idea, but she's wearing the same clothes she had on last night."

Misty cocked her head.

"That's what she wore during dinner," I added for clarification.

Misty scanned the lake. I followed her line of sight. Nothing looked out of place. The water was calm and smooth like glass. Not even a fisherman was out motoring around. It wasn't unusual to have a boat or two bobbing in the morning mist, especially with the campground on the other side of the lake. Witches liked camping and fishing on vacation as much as the next guy. But it was early and not quite the weekend when the campground would be full.

"No wayward boats," Misty remarked.

"No boats at all."

"Which means it wasn't an accident."

I put the pieces together. "Because you don't accidentally drown fully clothed thirty feet from shore."

"Right. If Sophia fell off a boat, where's the boat?"

My eyes instantly went to the rowboats and canoes the inn made available for guests. Every one of them was pulled safely on the beach or hanging on the rack. In my head, I tried to picture a scenario of Sophia walking along the trail, tripping and hitting her head, ending up in the water and drowning. It seemed unlikely but not impossible. Not sure how she ended up that far away from shore, though, or if that part was even possible. I wasn't a forensics expert.

Unfortunately, I couldn't air my thoughts as Amber decided to interrupt our tête-à-tête.

"The guilty collaborating once more?"

"What is your problem? Did your mother not love you enough as a child?" Misty shot back, her eyes full of pity. Where I, on the other hand, had to bite my tongue and swallow my retort down like a jagged pill.

Amber pressed on. "What, did you think it would help drive visitors to your little festival?"

I couldn't hide the disgusted expression on my face at Amber's vile accusation. The festival was the last thing on my mind. I couldn't keep my mouth shut any longer. "Seriously, what is your problem? You have issues, and I don't care who your daddy is or what badge you wear. You need to stop." I was about to say more, but my tongue got tied when I spotted Vance heading down the path behind me. He wore a tan business suit and brown leather loafers. His face was freshly shaven, and a gold watch donned his wrist. Clearly, he hadn't been out for a run.

"You okay?" he asked when he reached me, taking in my disheveled appearance—dripping wet, missing a shoe, mascara probably running down my face.

Amber rolled her eyes but didn't say anything.

"What are you doing here?" I couldn't help blurting out.

Vance took my outburst in stride. "I was down at the station when the call came in. As soon as I heard Mystic Inn, I headed this way. You're okay then?" The question was nonchalant, but the look in Vance's eyes was not. He was worried about me. I read it plain as day on his face.

I took a steadying breath. "I am, but Sophia's not." I motioned over to where Deputy Jones and Dr. Fitz stood. The doctor covered Sophia's body with a white sheet.

"What happened?" Vance asked.

"I think I'll be the one asking the questions," Amber interrupted, puffing out her chest like a proud peacock.

I looked at Amber and raised my eyebrows, waiting for her to continue. We all did.

Amber pulled her phone out of her pocket, opened an app, and held it out the way a reporter holds out a microphone during an interview. "So, tell me, what did happen?"

I rubbed my shoulder and looked to Vance to see if he thought I should continue. He was, after all, a defense attorney and knew how Amber liked to twist my words. If he thought I should keep my mouth shut, he would tell me, but if anything, Vance looked like he wanted to know the answer just as much as Amber.

"Well, I was walking down the trail to meet Misty. We were planning to go for a run this morning when I saw Sophia." I looked back over to the sheet and wondered if it was possible to bleach the memory from my brain, or better yet, ask Aunt Thelma to spell it away.

"That's it?" Amber pulled her phone back and looked down at the screen. I could see my words appear on the dictating app. She thrust the phone back into my face.

"That's it. At first, I thought it was a lifejacket, but as soon as I realized it was a person, I ran out into the lake to help, but Sophia was long gone." One look at her bloated body, and it was apparent she had been in the water some time.

Deputy Jones joined us at that moment and handed me a blanket. I wrapped the gray fleece around myself. I hadn't even realized I had been shivering.

"What about you?" Amber asked Misty.

"I heard Angelica shout for help. It took me probably a minute or less to reach her. That's when I called you guys," Misty replied.

"Convenient," Amber replied under her breath.

"Do you have any other questions," Vance asked, snapping into lawyer mode.

"Sophia was staying at the inn, wasn't she?" Amber asked.

"She was. She and her husband checked in early yesterday," I confirmed.

"Bet you loved that," Amber replied with a smirk, knowing the inn was far from ready to receive guests.

I shrugged, not giving Amber the satisfaction of knowing she was right. "Sophia was a close friend of my aunt. Speaking of which, I should go talk to her."

"Good idea." Amber tucked her phone back in her pocket. "You can show me Sophia's room on the way."

"Sure, I'll lead the way," I mumbled. The sinking feeling returned to my chest.

CHAPTER SIX

The walk back to the inn was a somber one. I wasn't looking forward to breaking the news to Sophia's loved ones. It didn't help that a crow seemed to follow after us, circling high in the air with its foreboding caw.

"What in the world is going on out there? And why are you all wet?" Aunt Thelma asked when we trooped in together.

My aunt's face fell when she spotted Amber strut in behind us like she owned the place. It was never good news when Deputy Reynolds stepped foot inside Mystic Inn.

"What? What is it? What's wrong?" Aunt Thelma's eyes darted amongst the group.

I didn't even try to hide my expression.

"Who is it? What happened?" Aunt Thelma continued to pepper the air with questions.

I took a steadying breath.

"You're right, something's happened. There's been an accident." I pulled my aunt aside to break the rest of the news to her upstairs in private, and where I could also change.

"Sophia's dead? Wonder what on earth happened," Aunt Thelma blinked and looked at me for more information. That wasn't the reaction I was expecting.

It took me a moment to reply.

"I'm honestly not sure. Did you see Sophia this morning?" I cautiously asked.

"No, but that's not unusual. Sophia always liked to sleep in."

"What about last night?" I asked while slipping a clean shirt over my head.

"I left her and Arthur at the lake." Aunt Thelma looked off in the distance. "Wonder how he's taking it?"

"I suppose we should go downstairs and find out. Just let me finish getting ready."

The words were barely out of my mouth, and Aunt Thelma whipped out her wand. Before I could protest, she pointed the wand at my face and uttered a glamour charm. In a snap, my face was bright and fresh as a spring daisy.

"Or, you could do that." I checked out my reflection in the mirror. My eyes shone like emeralds, and my complexion was radiant. I blinked once or twice to make sure I saw myself clearly.

"Come on, dear, let's go." Aunt Thelma patted my arm.

Downstairs, Percy and Amber were creating a scene, bickering back and forth like school children.

"Stop that! I'll arrest you!" Amber swatted at the spitballs that Percy shot her way.

"Na-na na-na boo-boo, you can't stop me," Percy sang back.

"Oh yes, I can," Amber withdrew her wand.

"Are you going to tell her you can't curse a ghost, or should I?" Vance said under his breath to Misty.

"I need to know what room was Sophia's. Are you going to help me or not?" Amber demanded with her wand raised threatening over her shoulder. One flick of her wrist and a spell would shoot out from the tip.

"Not!" Percy blew a raspberry and disappeared into the ether.

"I can show you!" I quickly intervened before Amber blasted a hole where Percy once stood. "Right this way," I motioned for the deputy to follow me. Amber glared at the spot where Percy had been standing moments before.

"I assigned her two adjoining rooms seeing none of the suites are ready yet," I explained.

Amber moved to follow me, but we were interrupted by Deputy Jones. "Deputy Reynolds, a word." Deputy Jones motioned with two fingers for Amber to join him in the lobby entryway. In his hand was a plastic bag with a length of rope in it. I wasn't sure what it meant at first, but thanks to the echo in the open lobby, everything the deputies said carried our way.

"Rope tied around her ankle?" Amber repeated.

"My guess is someone tied her down to something. Maybe a rock or a weight, but it didn't hold," Deputy Jones speculated.

Misty's eyebrows shot up. She looked at me knowingly. There went my accidental drowning theory. I hadn't even had a chance to share it with anyone.

"This wasn't an accident," Amber said. Deputy Jones shook his head no.

"What was that room number?" Amber marched back in my direction, determination locked on her face.

"Room 104," I stepped back as Deputy Jones joined Amber, and they headed down the hall. A moment later, we heard the knock on the door.

"Did you forget your key?" Arthur said as he opened the door. "Oh, sorry. I thought you were Sophia."

"And when was the last time you saw Sophia?" Amber asked, jumping right to it.

"Um...ah...I," Arthur stammered, realizing something wasn't right. "Last night when I went to bed."

"Was she also in bed?" Amber asked.

"What? Uh, no. Separate rooms. I snore. Drives Sophia nuts." Arthur chuckled. "Is something wrong? Is Sophia okay?"

"How do you know something's happened to Sophia?" Amber got into Arthur's face.

Arthur took a step back, "Um, because of your questioning?"

"Nice try, buddy," Amber shot back.

Deputy Jones intervened. "Sir, there's been an incident. We'd like to talk with you outside." Deputy Jones's voice managed to inflict compassion and authority at the same time. Unlike his coworker, Deputy Jones wasn't jumping to any conclusions.

"Something has happened to her, hasn't it?" Arthur wasn't hysterical but rather curious.

"Yes, something has. Sophia was found dead this morning in the lake. Now please get your things and come with us." Amber's attitude was night and day compared to Deputy Jones's.

"Sophia's dead?" Arthur repeated, as if making sure he heard Amber correctly.

"I'm sorry," Deputy Jones replied, sounding like he meant it.

"Huh." Arthur stood there, looking out in space before finally saying, "I'll get my things."

Within a handful of minutes, Arthur and the deputies left.

"Well, that was odd," Misty said as soon as they were outside the door.

"Yeah, that's not how I expected Arthur to react at all," I confessed.

"He could have been in shock," Vance supplied.

"I guess." I wasn't sure what shock looked like.

"I'm not buying it." Misty pointed at Vance. "How would you react if they found Angelica in the lake like that?"

My eyes went wide.

Before I could say anything, Vance replied, "You're right. Not like that." Misty looked at me. A smug expression on her face. As if now was the time and place to be reminded of my history with Vance. "Do you think Arthur has something to do with it?"

"I don't know. It would've had to have happened last night. She wore the same thing at dinner." I directed the last of the comment to Vance. "When I left, she was talking with Aunt Thelma and Arthur." I turned to see what Aunt Thelma thought, but she was occupied putting on a pot of coffee. She generally put on a pot before the construction crew arrived. This morning wasn't any different. She even hummed a cheerful tune while she did it. "Speaking of acting odd." I motioned to my aunt.

Misty shrugged her shoulders as if to say, beats me. Vance furrowed his brow.

"I guess everyone processes grief differently," I surmised. "Anyway, I wonder if Percy saw anything during the night shift." I should've thought to ask him right away. "Hey, Percy!" I yelled into the empty lobby. "Per-cy!" I cupped my hands to my mouth and shouted, the way a person calls their dog when they've wandered a bit too far away.

"Yes, Jelly?" The poltergeist had called me Jelly for as long as I could remember. Most people shortened Angelica to Angie or Angela, but not Percy.

"Hey, did you see Sophia leave last night?"

"Maaay-be." Percy rocked back on his heels.

"Percy, c'mon. This is serious. Did you see Sophia leave last night or not?" I tried not to keep my voice level, but failed a bit.

"I'm not going to tell you if you keep talking to me like that." Percy folded his transparent arms across his chest and put his nose in the air like a petulant child.

I took a deep breath.

"I'm sorry, Percy. You're right." I cleared my throat. "Could you be so kind as to do us this one favor? It would be very nice of you, and I'd greatly appreciate it." My voice was sweeter than molasses, and I laid it on just as thick.

"How much would you appreciate it?" Percy looked down.

"A whole bunch. Wouldn't we guys?" I eyed Vance and Misty to agree.

"Oh yeah, a bunch," Vance said, nodding.

Misty rolled her eyes but then agreed as well.

"Enough to get me a piece of fudge from the candy shop?" Percy asked.

"What do you want that for? You can't eat it." Misty replied matter-of-factly.

I elbowed my friend in her ribs and eyed her to shut it. If Percy wanted a piece of fudge, I'd get him a piece of fudge.

"But I can smell it. And smelling it is almost as good as eating it." Percy looked down at Misty and schooled her on his ghostly ways.

"Right, okay. Yes. One piece of fudge coming up. But first, can you tell us what you saw last night?" I made sure to keep the kindness in my voice.

"Well, tell you the truth, I did see Sophia. 'Course, I

didn't think anything of it. She left around nine o'clock."

"Was she alone?" Misty asked.

"I would've told you if she wasn't," Percy replied, clearly still annoyed with Misty for questioning his fudge request.

"Did anyone else come or go?" I asked.

"Like Arthur?" Vance added.

"No. Just her. Then again, I wasn't expecting anyone, and I was watching my show," Percy said.

"Your show?" Misty asked.

"Lifestyles of the Witch and Famous," I answered for Percy. He loved seeing how upper-class witches lived.

Percy nodded. "But I'll let you know if I see her ghost kicking around."

"Oh...thanks." I guess. I hadn't thought of that, but if Sophia's ghost were here, that would make solving her case easy (that is, if she could remember what happened to her).

Percy didn't wait for us to ask him any more questions before winking out of existence.

"What a strange little man," Misty said.

"I heard that!" Percy's detached voice replied from across the lobby.

I shook my head, dismissing Percy from my thoughts.

"So, Sophia left alone around nine o'clock," Misty summarized.

"Maybe she went for a walk?" I suggested.

"Or maybe she was meeting up with someone," Vance said.

I snapped my fingers. "Like that guy from the book-store yesterday."

"Yes!" Misty's eyes lit up like I was on to something.

"What guy?" Vance had no idea what we were talking about.

"Rick Kelly," Misty supplied.

"He threatened her, didn't he?" I tried to think back to what he said.

Misty nodded her head. "Something about exposing her as a fraud."

"Right. And then, last night, Sophia was arguing with someone on the phone. It sounded like they were threatening her, too."

"Do you think it was Rick again?" Misty asked.

"That would make the most sense," I surmised.

"What's this? Someone murdered Sophia Emerson? And in my town?" Mayor Parish walked into the lobby in a flourish. Her hands were in the air, bent at the elbow, as her fingers grasped the air for answers. "This is all your fault," she rounded on me.

"Excuse me?" I replied.

"Are you crazy?" Misty shot back at the same time.

Vance, who had been leaning against the registration desk, stood up, ready to interject. His eyes darkened as Mayor Parrish continued.

"Oh, you said so yourself. This fall festival was your idea. Sophia would have never dreamed of coming home this weekend if you hadn't lured her in."

"I didn't lure her in. Sophia jumped at the opportunity," I snapped. I had a feeling it was more to help Aunt Thelma than the festival itself, but that was beside the point.

Mayor Parish ignored my comment.

"This murder is going to put us on the map for entirely the wrong reason!" Mayor Parish punctuated the air with her finger. Her voice turned shrill.

"It is not—" I clamped my mouth shut, unable to finish my sentence because the mayor was right. I had been replying automatically before thinking about what I was saying. This was going to put Silverlake on the map for the wrong reason. I had planned to drum up business for Silverlake and turn its reputation around. The murder of a celebrity was the last thing we needed.

"You need to fix this. Quickly. Until then, I have work to do." Mayor Parrish turned on her heel. "As do you." The mayor looked around the dismantled lobby, careful not to touch anything for fear she might get dust on her dress.

It was hard to tell if she meant fixing Sophia's murder or the inn by her judgmental parting look.

"Well, then." Misty raised her eyebrows.

I swallowed uncomfortably. My mouth felt dry. "She's right, though. Not that we can fix what happened to Sophia, but we can help solve her murder."

Not to mention that Sophia deserved justice, and Deputy Reynolds, sure as a witch's hat was black, wasn't going to deliver it. Deputy Jones tried to keep her in line, but when your daddy's the sheriff, you can pretty much get away with whatever you want.

I glanced over at my aunt. The work crew had started to roll in. She greeted each one of them with a smile and an offer of coffee. I let out a puff of air. Aunt Thelma might be acting cool at the moment, but I'd bet anything she was in denial. The same for Arthur. It was the most logical explanation. They say denial is not just a river in Egypt, but right now, those two were taking a pleasure cruise down the longest river in the world. However, I had a feeling that once the reality of the situation set in, they'd want us to step up and help. I know if someone murdered a friend of mine, and it was up to Deputy Reynolds to solve, I'd want help too.

I said as much to Misty and Vance.

"Now you're talking," Misty's eyes sparkled with excitement. She loved taking down bad guys even more than I did.

"Maybe we can get lucky, close the case, and prevent Sophia's murder from becoming sensational-ized. Wrap things up as quickly as possible — but for the right reasons." I eyed Vance to see what he thought. But he'd tuned us out. He gazed at the ground, and I wondered what he was thinking.

My attention turned to Aunt Thelma. She went behind the counter to fetch the coffee pot. Out front, Benny's van pulled in. He almost always showed up after his crew. I took advantage of the moment to talk to Aunt Thelma before Benny required her attention.

"What do you know about Rick Kelly?" I asked as she took a sip of her coffee.

"He's not single if that's what you're asking." Aunt Thelma had a mischievous twinkle in her eye.

"What? No. Geez, Louise. Misty and I heard him threaten Sophia at the bookstore yesterday. I was wondering what the connection was there."

"He did?" Aunt Thelma looked into her coffee mug. Unlike me, she took her coffee with half a cup of creamer. Okay, maybe not that much, but she drank it more like a latte than a regular cup of joe. Aunt Thelma's brow wrinkled in concentration. "Let's see. Rick would be her nephew-in-law. He married Kayla, her niece — the last permanent Emerson resident after her mama and granny went up to heaven one right after the other."

"I'm sorry to hear that." I vaguely remembered the older Emerson women. The grandmother was the best baker in Silverlake. Maybe the skill skipped a generation, or maybe Sophia wasn't a fraud after all.

"Kayla was pretty torn up about it. Not that anyone could blame her," Aunt Thelma continued.

"No, I don't imagine they could." I knew all about losing your mama.

"But then she and Rick had a baby about nine months ago. She's been smiling ever since."

"Any idea where they live?"

"Last I knew, it was over in the apartments next to the high school. Sophia would've known for sure. I still can't believe she's dead."

"I know. Me either."

Aunt Thelma sighed and then took a sip of her coffee. After a quiet moment she said, "Well, I guess I better go see what Benny's up to today." Aunt Thelma topped off her coffee cup, filled a second mug, and walked over to hand it to the contractor. I cocked my head as I watched her talk to Benny as if today was an ordinary day. My aunt was acting odd indeed, no talking about Sophia's suspicious death or encouraging me to investigate. She didn't even talk about suspects or motives. *Denial*, I reminded myself and promised to give my aunt time to process the loss.

I rejoined Misty and Vance. "I found out where Rick lives. Sort of. He's married to Kayla, Sophia's niece. Aunt Thelma says they live in the apartments by the high school. I'm going to check it out."

"I'll come with you. Just let me run back to open the store up and tell Vicki where I'll be." Misty bent low to the ground and retied her shoelace.

"You're taking the trail?" I'm pretty sure my mouth was hanging open.

"Sure, why not? I doubt the killer's going to jump out at me, and if they do, I'll have my wand at the ready." Misty winked. "I'll see you in thirty?"

"Sure." My voice lacked confidence.

That didn't matter because Misty hadn't waited for me reply. She'd already sidestepped the workmen and was walking toward the front door before the word left my lips.

"How is that rebellious witch my best friend?" I said on a sigh.

"Because you used to be a rebel too," Vance replied.

I furrowed my brow. "Ah, that's right." Maybe there was still a bit of that rebellious nature buried deep inside me. Very deep.

"I have court later this morning, but I can help after that."

"Yeah, that would be great." I could use all the help I could get. It was crazy to think how quickly Vance and I had become friends, and how *not* weird it was to hang out again. I reminded myself that that was a good thing, and showed how much we'd matured over the years.

I could tell Vance wanted to say something else in the ensuing silence, but he held back.

"What is it?" I prodded. I searched Vance's expression, trying to read him.

Vance looked me straight in the eye. "Do *you* have a game plan if the bad guy jumps out at you?"

Err... No, no I did not.

Luckily, I was good at thinking on my feet. I stood straight, shoulders back and head held high. "Of course. I'll just freeze the scumbag and call the cops," I proclaimed, proud of how confident I sounded. But then I thought for a moment. "Except..."

"What?"

"Except my cell phone took a swim this morning in the lake. I need to file an insurance claim and have a new one shipped before meeting back up with Misty."

"Okay, how about you do that, and then I'll give you a ride?"

I looked out the wall of windows and the lake beyond that. If I was honest, unlike Misty, I wasn't in any hurry to walk the Enchanted Trail again. It wasn't the first time the trail had caught me off guard, but that's another story. If my bad luck on the walking path kept up, I'd have to rename it something more fitting, like the Haunted Trail or the Dark Walk.

I had a rental car when I first arrived back in Silverlake, but that had only been good through the extended weekend. I'd been walking everywhere and borrowing my aunt's car ever since. Silverlake wasn't an overly large town, but a car did make things more convenient. A five-minute trip to the grocery store could take an hour or more on foot. I loved not having a car payment, but I also needed reliable transportation, and I couldn't depend on Vance always being ready to save the day. No, it was time I looked into purchasing a vehicle of my own, something that I hadn't needed to do in Chicago. But until then, I turned to Vance and said, "Yes, I'd love a ride."

"Okay. I'll be out working in my truck. Why don't you come on out when you're ready?"

I replied that I would at the same time a new guest walked into the lobby.

CHAPTER SEVEN

"Hello, is anybody here?" The woman gazed tentatively around the lobby. Her suitcase rolled behind her.

I took in the woman's appearance. She was a supernatural of some sort. If not, she would have glowed. It was a fact I had forgotten until my ex-boyfriend, Allen, had popped in for a visit. Mortals glowed ethereal-like in Silverlake. It was how witches knew not to perform magic in front of them.

"How can I help you?" I turned away from Vance and greeted the woman.

"Oh, thank goodness someone is here. Tell me it isn't true. Sophia's not really dead. She can't be. This is a publicity stunt, isn't it? I mean, she promised she wouldn't do that again. Well, not without telling me, but you know how Sophia is. That Sleep of the Dead is a tricky potion. Is she here?" The woman looked expectantly around the room as if Sophia was going to jump out and say Boo!

I hesitated before speaking, not sure of how to respond.

"I'm sorry, but yes, ma'am, it's true." It was Vance who'd replied. He stood beside me. His presence helped calm me more than I'd ever admit.

"What?" The woman's face fell. "Are you sure?" Her eyes darted between Vance and my face, looking for me to refute it.

"The police just left," I added, keeping the details vague. I still didn't know who this woman was.

The woman opened and shut her mouth twice as if looking for the right words and unsure what to say. She brought her hand to her mouth. "I don't know what to think. I'm in shock." She spoke through her fingers. "Sophia was full of so much life. How did this happen?" The woman's questions weren't rhetorical. She stared at us, looking for answers.

"I don't know. The deputies didn't say much." I eyed Vance to keep his mouth shut. This woman was setting off my witchy instincts left and right. "Were you friends with Sophia?" I looked down at the woman's luggage. They still had baggage claim tags around the handle, indicating she'd flown in.

"I'm sorry. Where's my head? Today's been too much. I'm Lorraine Bennings, Sophia's manager." Tears formed in the corner of the woman's eyes. She puffed out her cheeks and exhaled through pursed lips, like a woman trying to hold it together. Vance lifted the tissue box off the front counter and offered Lorraine one. She accepted, dabbing her eyes while she thanked him.

"I don't know what to do now. Where I should stay or what I need to do." Lorraine shook her head with a dazed expression fixed on her face.

Around us, the workmen got busy. They'd gone ahead and started installing the carpet. If the downstairs threads didn't match the upstairs, even with magic, so be it. We were doing the best we could.

Lorraine seemed to look past the workers, focusing on something else in the distance. "I was supposed to meet Sophia here on business. I'd just landed when my phone alerts went off," she added after a moment.

"You could stay here. I know it's currently a mess, but you're more than welcome," Aunt Thelma joined us with a broad smile on her face.

I hadn't seen my aunt come up behind me. She must've finished talking business with Benny.

"I'm sure Lorraine would like someplace quieter," I made an excuse for the woman. If Aunt Thelma would've looked at me, she'd see me staring her down. I don't know why, but I did not want Lorraine to stay here.

But Aunt Thelma didn't look up.

"This is where Sophia was staying?" Lorraine seemed unsure.

"Yes, we went way back," Aunt Thelma fluttered her hand in the air, indicating that it was a long time.

"Oh, I see. You must be Thelma." Lorraine pursed her lips.

"I am," Aunt Thelma beamed.

Seemingly making up her mind, Lorraine thrust her hand out. "Lorraine Benning. Sophia's manager." Lorraine pumped Aunt Thelma's hand up and down. "Or I was." She cleared her throat uncomfortably. "Perhaps you could tell me what happened?" Lorraine leaned forward, keeping her voice low as she fished for more information. It seemed she would love nothing more than to cart Aunt Thelma off for a private conversation.

Aunt Thelma didn't budge. "Oh, I don't really know much. I try and stay out of police business. The deputies did take Arthur in, so I suppose that's something."

I shot my aunt an expression that said, "Would you please be quiet?!"

This time she caught my eye and replied with a shrug. Aunt Thelma wasn't picking up on the same vibe from Lorraine that I was.

"Now, that doesn't surprise me," Lorraine confessed.

"What's that supposed to mean?" I asked. Arthur seemed like a nice guy. He didn't set off my instincts the way this woman did.

"Arthur was always jealous of Sophia. Couldn't handle being in her shadow. That's probably why he cheated on her." Lorraine looked down, examining her fingernails as if this was old news.

"Cheated on her? Really?" Aunt Thelma looked

surprised. It was the first sign of emotion I had seen on her all day.

"It made him feel like a man." Lorraine deepened her voice on the last word and puffed out her chest, making her seem more masculine. "Or at least that's what I always figured."

"I don't know. They looked the picture of happiness last night," I quipped.

Lorraine ignored me. "I don't know what Sophia ever saw in him. I told her he would be the death of her, and it looks like I was right. She should've listened to me and dumped him years ago. Now I can't even tell her I told you so. What a tragedy." Lorraine sighed, sounding like it was anything but. "At least it sounds like your sheriff's smart."

I replied with a fake smile. I wasn't going there. Vance grinned at my expression.

"I still don't know what I should do, though." Lorraine appeared to weigh her options. Her eyes looked up at the ceiling.

"If you'd like, we could hold your bags for you until you decide," Aunt Thelma offered.

"Could you do that?" Lorraine looked at me to respond.

"Oh, sure. No problem at all." Because, really, what else was I supposed to say?

"I have another one in the car. Let me go grab it. I'll be just a minute."

Our trio watched as Lorraine walked out of the inn's lobby.

"I don't know, Aunt Thelma. I don't think it's a good idea having anyone stay here. We don't even know who she is, and with Sophia's death..." I let my words hang in the air. "I don't know," I repeated. It seemed to be the only thing I could say.

"You worry too much, dear. I'm sure it'll be fine." Aunt Thelma reached over and patted me on the shoulder before turning away and making her way back to the coffee station.

"Maybe she's right," Vance said, trying to be helpful.

"And maybe she's not," I replied, refusing to ignore my instincts. "Come on, let's go. I'll worry about my phone later."

CHAPTER EIGHT

So much for keeping the case under wraps. A Witch News Network van was parked right in front of Wishing Well Park. It was a dang shame that the network's headquarters were in Atlanta. In the hour since the news broke, the network was already on site. It was as if WNN had set up shop at the festival's registration desk. Lead anchor, Starry Evans, held a microphone to her mouth and spoke directly into the camera.

"How much do you want to bet she's not covering the fall festival?" Vance pulled into a parking spot and surveyed the scene.

I didn't reply. I was doing the same and wondering what on earth I was going to do about it all. Make that, wondering what I *could* do about it. Everything that'd happened lately was out of my hands, and yet I still wanted to try and fix it—the inn, Sophia's death, the festival—it felt like a losing battle.

"Ange?" Vance turned and looked at me when I didn't reply.

"Sorry. I was trying to think if I could magick Starry Evans away."

"Her and her thousands of viewers." Vance looked back at Starry. She had roped Mr. McCormick in for an interview. He shifted his weight side-to-side, rocking back and forth uncomfortably as if he was ready to walk out of the frame without a moment's notice.

I grimaced.

"This is bad, Vance. I don't want Silverlake to be known as the town where someone murdered Sophia Emerson. You know that's what's going to happen. Pretty soon, tours will pop up, highlighting where Sophia grew up, retracing her last twenty-four hours, that sort of thing."

"That's not going to happen." But Vance didn't sound confident.

"Have you ever been to LA? They have O.J. Simpson tours, Marilyn Monroe tours, Charles Manson tours. I could go on. People love tragedy."

Vance thought for a moment while watching the action outside of the van. Starry motioned to one of the tents over her shoulder while still addressing her audience. Mr. McCormick inched back. "Okay, maybe you're right. People's morbid curiosity will bring them to Silverlake, but that's not what will keep them here and keep them coming back. We have an opportunity here."

"An opportunity?" I wasn't so sure, and the hesitation in my voice showed it.

"To showcase Silverlake's charm. Sophia's death isn't going to define our community or us. Silverlake's unique."

"True, but—"

Vance kept talking. "Trust me. Our town welcomes everyone with open arms. It's a place where we can be ourselves and let our magic fly. Tell me, where else will you find a place like that? I'll tell you, nowhere."

"Maybe." Vance did have a point, but I wasn't sure if Silverlake's charm was enough to overcome Sophia's death, not after it was sensationalized.

"Silverlake puts everyone under its spell. You'll see."

"I don't know."

"It brought you home, didn't it? You're just what this town needs." Vance winked.

I coughed hard.

"You okay?"

"Yeah, just a tickle." I choked the words out.

"Trust me. I know if anyone can turn this around, it's you."

Again, with the compliment. I cleared my throat. Tears swam in my eyes as I tried not to cough some more. Wasn't I just saying how normal it was hanging out and now I was reacting like this? What was wrong with me? I don't know why Vance's kind words affected me so much. I don't know why his praise meant so much. I don't know why I even cared.

I sighed and realized that I don't know why I try and lie to myself.

Because maybe, just maybe it was because there was so much water under the bridge that sometimes I'd felt like I was going to drown. Maybe it's because there was something still there between us after all these years.

Whatever it was, I didn't want to think about it.

I changed the subject.

"Have you ever thought about running for mayor?"

"It was a good speech, wasn't it?"

"I believed you. I can see why you're good at your job." I looked around. Wishing Well Park looked ready for the festival, but the surrounding shops, not so much. There wasn't a single pumpkin, haystack, or decorative leaf to be spotted. Not to mention some of the store-front windows could use a good washing. "If we're going to change people's minds, we're going to have to step up our efforts."

"What are you thinking?" Vance followed my line of sight.

I bit my bottom lip while thinking. "What about a business decorating contest? We could offer cash prizes for whatever businesses embody the essence of Silver-lake the best."

"How much cash?"

"That depends on how many businesses enter. I'll throw in a hundred bucks to kick it off. Then we can add a fifteen-dollar registration fee. Business owners will have to drop it off with their entry form."

"There's an entry form?"

"There will be by this afternoon. I'll design it and print it out after running it by the committee. I can drop copies off at Village Square, too."

I looked across the park at the festival grounds.

"You don't think the festival itself has anything to do with Sophia's murder, do you?" My stomach clenched, and guilt washed over me at the prospect. I looked to Vance, hoping he could erase the fears.

"Honestly, it might."

"That wasn't what you were supposed to say!"

"All I mean is that the festival just gave him a chance."

"So, it is my fault," I mumbled with my hand on the truck's inside handle, ready to open the door and step out.

"I didn't say that." Vance reached across the center console and touched his hand to my leg. It wasn't a romantic gesture. It was more of a move to make his point. "You're not responsible for somebody else's choices. This festival was a good idea. I wasn't joking when I said this town needs you."

I replied with a weak smile and slipped out of the car.

"I should be done around one o'clock if you want to meet up then," Vance said to me as I stood in the doorway with my hand on the truck's frame.

"Sounds good. Give me a call." I moved to shut the door. "Uh, I mean, I'll call you around one, and we can figure it out." Stupid cell phone. I needed to do something about that, stat.

"Okay. And Angie? Be careful."

I replied with a curt nod and then did shut the door.

Misty was behind the checkout counter scribbling something down on a piece of paper when I entered the bookstore. Her eyes darted between the computer screen and back down to what she was writing.

"You ready?" I asked.

"Yes, and I have Kayla's address." Misty proudly held up the scrap piece of paper. "She signed up for the store's mailing list."

"Aren't you clever."

"And you'll never guess who our customer of the month is."

"Kayla Kelly?"

"You got it. And it's not like I don't know her. She comes in here all the time. I think she's read every book we have on pregnancy and baby's first year. I expect she'll be hitting the toddler section soon and dropping in for storytime."

"Nice." I wasn't about to turn down having a cover. In fact, I hadn't even thought of one. I suppose I had planned on just jumping right into it and seeing if Rick was home and questioning him. Misty's approach was smarter.

"If anyone deserves to be customer of the month, it's Kayla." Misty slipped the gift card into an envelope, tucked in the flap, and then wrote Kayla's name on the front in an elegant script. She then reached below the counter for a merchandise bag. Misty opened the brown bag, dropped the gift card inside, and then walked over to a display table, plucking the week's featured read off the table and adding it to the bag.

"Now we're ready. I just need to be back in an hour. Vicki has a dentist appointment."

"Hopefully, it won't even take that long."

The apartments by the high school were comprised of three units, each three stories tall and all outfitted with gray siding, black shutters, and heavy white front doors. A business office stood off to the right-hand side of the property with a playground tucked behind it. We stopped at the stop sign inside the complex.

"That way, right?" Misty nodded with her head to the left.

I went to agree, but then I spotted Kayla. At least, I was pretty sure that's who it was. I pointed to the young woman at the park. She had pulled her bright blonde hair high up in a ponytail. I watched as she pushed the young child in one of the two baby swings. The little one giggled when her mama pushed her.

"Yep, that's her and Ava." Misty turned right and pulled in a spot in front of the business office.

Kayla was unclipping Ava from the swing by the time we reached her.

"You ready for a ba-ba and a nap?" She cooed to her little one as she scooped her up. The babe clutched onto a handful of Kayla's hair and yanked, giggling the entire time.

"What did I say about pulling mommy's hair?" Kayla didn't sound put out one bit. In fact, she smiled the entire time.

"Hey, Kayla," Misty interrupted.

"Oh!" Kayla jumped in surprise.

"Sorry, didn't mean to scare you," Misty said.

"That's okay. Rick's always telling me I don't pay attention. Maybe he's right. But don't tell him I said that. Your daddy thinks he's always right," Kayla said the last part to her daughter. "But your mama knows a thing or two."

I smiled at the exchange and caught Kayla's eye.

"I'm Angelica. Not sure if you remember me." I waved from the side.

"Thelma's niece," Kayla nodded.

"Mm-hm." I nodded the acknowledgment.

"Are you looking for an apartment? I think they've got first month free right now." Kayla looked over to the office. I followed her line of sight. Sure enough, a sign out front advertised the promotion. Purple flags waved around it, drawing attention to the deal.

"Actually, we're looking for you." Misty held the gift bag out. "You're Spell Binding's customer of the month! Thought I'd drop it off in person."

"Oh, well, isn't that something. I've never won anything before. You just made my day." Kayla took the gift bag with one hand and juggled the baby on her hip.

"We also wanted to pay our respects. I'm sorry about your aunt," I added as an afterthought.

"What's that now?" Kayla cocked her head and was

waiting for more of an explanation. It was apparent she didn't know about Sophia.

"Um." I swallowed uncomfortably. It was foolish of me to assume Kayla knew about her aunt. Just because WNN was blasting it all over the news didn't mean Kayla had heard, especially if she'd spent the morning at the playground.

"I'm sorry, I thought that you already knew." I tried to backtrack.

Kayla looked to me for details, but I didn't know what to say. My tongue felt thick as if I'd been cursed, and my mouth was suddenly dryer than the Sahara.

"Sophia was found in the lake this morning. She drowned last night," Misty stepped in and said.

"Oh my gosh." The air seemed to rush out of Kayla's lungs, and her shoulders sagged.

I reached forward and offered to take the baby from her. Kayla obliged.

"Hi, princess. Aren't you a doll." I smiled down at the little girl. She was the spitting image of her mama.

"I can't believe it," Kayla added.

Misty led Kayla over to the park bench. The two sat down together. I stood close by, entertaining Ava with coos and smiles. The little girl reached up and locked onto a handful of my hair. She happily yanked and babbled. "You're like a snapping turtle, aren't you? You're never going to let go." I teased the little one.

"You said she drowned? How?" Kayla asked Misty.

"We don't really know much," Misty confessed.

Which wasn't the complete truth. We didn't know

everything, but we knew more than we were saying. Kayla seemed upset enough. I didn't think we should offer up any gruesome details. As it was, the scene from this morning replayed in my mind often enough. I shivered, taking the vividness away and focused on the present.

"I'm shocked. I saw Sophia yesterday. She was here not twenty-four hours ago. My gosh. And what about Arthur?"

"He's talking with the sheriff right now," I confessed.

"The sheriff?" Kayla looked alarmed. Her head darted between Misty and me, looking for answers.

"They're trying to piece everything together. I'm sure it's standard procedure." My rationale sounded believable to my ears. But apparently not Ava's. The baby started fussing in my arms. "It's okay. Shhh-shhh-shhh." I turned my attention to the little one, but my efforts were futile. Ava began to wiggle and squirm. A defiant cry ripped from her lungs a moment later.

Kayla stood up. "It's okay, peanut." She took the baby from my arms and kissed the top of her head. Turning her attention to us, she said, "It's time for her nap. She's going to be a mess until I can get her down."

"Here, we'll walk back with you," Misty offered.

Kayla nodded, and after getting Ava settled into her stroller, we made our way back to the apartment.

Boy was Kayla right.

Ava raised cane the entire walk back. It didn't matter if Kayla carried her or pushed her in the stroller.

The little girl wasn't having it. Kayla tried to bribe Ava with a pacifier. She'd suckle once or twice, spit it back out, and start screaming once again. Kayla fished a fabric crinkle book out from the diaper bag, only to have Ava toss it over the side. Twice.

Thankfully it was a short walk.

Within five minutes of being back home, Ava was fast asleep.

"Whew," Kayla said, meeting us back in her kitchen.

Kayla's home was tidy. You didn't see any sticky countertops or baskets full of laundry sitting out here. No, everything was clean and put away except for a few toys scattered on the floor and baby gear tucked in the corners.

Instead of joining us at the kitchen table, the young mom got to work washing dishes. She used a handheld brush to scrub the baby bottles clean before inverting them on a drying rack. Kayla talked while she worked.

"I can't believe she's gone. Poor Arthur." It was the third or fourth time Kayla uttered the phrase.

I looked to Misty. I wanted to inquire about Rick and Sophia's relationship, but I wasn't sure how to approach the topic. I took a chance and asked, "Were you guys close?"

"We were working on it." Kayla turned the tap on and rinsed out another bottle.

With my attention on Kayla, I hadn't heard the front door open. It closed with a slam.

I flinched.

Misty stood, wand out in a defensive stance.

Kayla jumped, dropping the baby bottle in the water. Suds splashed up onto the counter.

"You got lunch ready?" Rick strutted forward. He stopped when he spotted us, his broad shoulders filling the doorframe. Rick's face settled into a scowl.

Misty tucked her wand away but still stood off to the side, ready to spring into action at a moment's notice.

"Shhh, the baby's sleeping," Kayla rushed forward to greet her husband, drying her hands on a towel at the same time.

"The baby's always sleeping," Rick grumbled. He found his feet again and walked past us in the kitchen.

"And no, I don't. Not yet. We have company," Kayla said by way of introduction.

"What do you want? We don't need nothing, and we already found Jesus," Rick started in on us. He ducked his head in the fridge and pulled back with a beer. Using his hand, he twisted the cap off and chucked it into the sink. It plopped in the soapy water with the forgotten bottle.

Kayla frowned.

"Misty owns the bookstore—" she started to say.

"You thinking about finally getting a job?" Rick interrupted after taking a long pull of beer.

"We actually stopped to pay our respects." Misty didn't bother to hide the irritation in her voice.

Rick scoffed. Sophia's death was no surprise to him.

"You knew about Sophia?" Kayla's eyes filled with hurt.

"Who don't? There's a news van blasting it everywhere." Rich chuckled darkly.

"What?" Kayla wasn't following.

"Starry Evans is broadcasting from Wishing Well Park," I explained.

Kayla visibly paled.

"Is there anyone you'd like us to call? Any family members?" I offered.

Kayla shook her head. "No, that's okay. I'll take care of it."

As if on cue, Kayla's cell phone rang. Kayla reached into her back pocket and answered the call. From the sounds of the conversation, it was someone calling to pay their respects. Kayla excused herself and walked the short distance to the living room.

Misty looked at me, and I could tell she was asking if I wanted to take the lead or if she should. We might not get another chance to talk to Rick alone.

I cleared my throat and took a chance. "Did you see Sophia yesterday? Kayla said she stopped by."

Rick downed the rest of his beer and finished with a scowl on his face. "That woman had no business here," he bit back.

"Is that what you were fighting about at the bookstore?" Misty's voice was innocent enough, but Rick's features turned darker. I thought maybe I should stand up too—before the predator pounced. Because at that moment, that was exactly what Rick looked like with his hooded eyes, and I did not want to be his prey.

"What?" Kayla interrupted, looking confused. She stood in the open doorway that separated the kitchen from the living room.

So much for having a private moment with Rick.

"You two fought yesterday?" Kayla only had eyes for her husband.

"I come home. She's been here. You're angry and upset. Of course, I'm going to have it out with the woman." Rick took a pull on the empty bottle and brought it down with annoyance on his face. He slammed the bottle on the counter.

I stood, thinking now would be a good time to go.

"Where were you last night?" Misty asked, goading Rick. I thought that was a wrong move, but Misty looked cool and calm. Probably because she actually knew how to use her wand if it came to it. I repeated the spell to freeze someone, glacio, under my breath. It had become my go-to spell when things got dicey, which it could at any moment.

"That's none of your business." Rick bit off.

"You don't think Rick had something to do with Sophia's death? It was an accident, wasn't it? You didn't say she was murdered," Kayla's voice hitched at the last word. Fear flooded her eyes. I wasn't sure if it was because she thought her husband was or wasn't capable of such a crime.

"You need to leave. Now!" Rick bellowed.

I flinched.

Upstairs, Ava woke with a piercing cry.

Kayla closed her eyes and sighed. I could see the weariness wash over her.

Rick turned away and ran his hand through his hair in frustration.

"Again, I'm sorry about your aunt." I met Kayla's eyes with a soft smile. My expression was as sympathetic as I could make it, given the situation.

Rick whipped back around, cutting my comment short with his frosty glare.

"Give me a call if you need anything," Misty added as we showed ourselves out the front door.

"Well, that went well." Misty's voice was heavy with sarcasm as we walked back to her car.

"At least Rick's not lying."

"No, you're right. He openly hated Sophia."

"Which means he probably didn't kill her."

"Because he's got nothing to hide?" Misty guessed.

"Exactly. If he were guilty, you'd think he would try and hide it. Wouldn't you?"

"One would think."

"Which means we're back to square one."

CHAPTER NINE

Misty and I parted ways at the entrance of the bookstore. Misty headed in to work, and I walked the short distance to La Luna to pick up a coffee and a pumpkin muffin, which was more like a cupcake with the cream cheese frosting piped in the middle of it. But instead of sitting inside the bakery and chatting with Diane and the locals, I took my treat to go, preferring to sit on a park bench alone with my thoughts. This morning had provided enough information to ruminate over for hours, if not days. Too bad I didn't have days to get to the bottom of it.

I sat and sipped my coffee, mentally creating a list of suspects. Rick was still on the list, but he'd dropped down a notch if only because he didn't hide anything. I'd never heard of a killer openly showing his disgust for the victim after the fact. Not while they were still presumed innocent, that is.

Then there was Lorraine. Sophia's business

manager rubbed me the wrong way, that much was true, but what if she'd been telling the truth about Arthur? Last night I only saw a snapshot of the couple's love life, and while I'd like to believe my impression was correct, and the two had been deeply in love, someone, in fact, had murdered Sophia. I would be remiss not to look into Arthur's whereabouts yesterday. If someone saw him at the local hardware buying rope and a brick, that would be a big red flag.

I thought back to what time Sophia arrived at the inn yesterday. It was early afternoon. Sophia had said that Arthur was golfing with Mike McCormick. That was a lead I could follow up on. Mr. McCormick was probably at the festival grounds right now. Not only was he overseeing the stage installation, but his greenhouse was also providing the hay bales, pumpkins, and decorative mums. Mayor Parrish might not have been too happy with the festival, but the town council was putting in more than their fair share of work. Or maybe I shouldn't give all the council members accolades and save my praise solely for Mr. McCormick. He was doing the work of three council members combined.

I tore off pieces of muffin and popped them in my mouth while deciding if anyone else was suspect. Who were Sophia's friends? Or better yet, her enemies? Surely, she had them even if they were unknown to me.

And herein lay the problem.

The fact of the matter was, I didn't know that much about Sophia. She didn't come to town all that often. As far as I knew, she had only dropped in a time or two the entire thirteen years I'd lived in Chicago. I should ask Aunt Thelma more about Sophia. Perhaps we could piece together a motive. That was if my aunt was up for it. It was easier for me to plow forward, tackling this case head-on because I wasn't blinded by grief. That was the only explanation for my aunt's blasé behavior. I tried to remember the five stages of grief, but I couldn't remember what came after denial. Was it anger, or did that come after depression? I suppose I could look back at my losses and try and sort it out, but that task didn't seem all that pleasant. Often times a wayward thought of my mama brought me to tears, and it had been years since I lost her. Diving into that grief was always painful.

No, it was best to keep my eyes forward. And right now, that meant talking to Mr. McCormick. Then later tonight, I'd see if Aunt Thelma was up for a chat.

I tossed the wax bakery bag my muffin had come in into the trash but kept my coffee to sip on as I snaked down Village Square's walking path and headed toward the park.

Outside of the candy shop, Luke waved as I approached. He swept the shop's entrance while his red-headed twin nieces, Beatrice and Sabrina, ran around out front, throwing woodchips from the front flower beds and shrieking at one another. Those girls were troublemakers if I ever saw one. The twins were old enough to know better, but that never seemed to stop them. It looked as if Luke was getting ready to decorate the front of his shop for fall if the pumpkins and brightly-colored leaf garland coiled up at his feet were any indications. Luke didn't need a business decorating competition to get him in the festival spirit. Hopefully, he'd enter it anyway, which reminded me that I needed to make up the entry form and run them by the committee before our meeting this afternoon.

I glanced down at my watch to check the hour, looking up just in time to see Beatrice almost plow right into Mrs. Potts. My second-grade teacher might've been advancing in age, but she was still light on her feet and was able to sidestep the rambunctious kiddo.

"Sorry, Mrs. Potts!" The young girl shouted.

"Sabrina." Luke's voice was full of calm condemnation.

"I said sorry!" Sabrina whined back.

"Where do you want this one, Uncle Luke?" Beatrice wisely abandoned the wood chips and had hoisted a giant pumpkin against her chest. She wobbled under its weight.

Luke dropped the broom and rushed over to help his niece.

"Let's set that down right here before it knocks you over." Luke caught my eye. "Morning. How's it going?"

I stopped. "Good. How's it going with you?"

"Eh," Luke shrugged his shoulders, taking in the craziness. "Parent-teacher conferences," Luke explained.

"Ah, so no school." I was wondering why the girls were off on a Wednesday.

Luke nodded. "My sister should be back soon."

"You're a good brother. You know that, right?" Luke's sister Sally was a single mom and nurse at the local community hospital. From the way Luke explained it, she picked up overtime every chance she got, leaving Luke to care for his nieces. Not that he ever complained. Sally and the girls were all Luke had, and vice versa.

"So, she tells me all the time," Luke replied with a boyish grin. "How's the festival?"

"The festival's fine. It's everything else that's a mess."

"I heard about Sophia." Luke was careful to keep his voice low, lest his nieces hear.

"Yeah, it's horrible," I cast my eyes down, still not believing someone murdered Sophia.

"Thelma's close with her, isn't she? I mean, I heard she was staying at the inn." Luke bobbed his head from side to side.

I knew what he meant. The inn wasn't accepting visitors, so if Sophia was staying there, she had to be close to my aunt. "Yeah, they were friends since high school.

"Then I'm extra sorry. Give her my condolences, will you?"

"I will." I looked through the front window of the candy shop. The glass-faced display cases filled with their chocolatey goodness called to me. If I hadn't already eaten the pumpkin muffin, I would have answered it. Maybe next time, I told myself.

"Well, if you need anything, let me know. I'm free after five," Luke offered.

"Thanks. I really appreciate that. I'll see you later, okay?" I continued walking before stopping. "Percy's fudge!" I snapped my fingers.

"Pardon me?" Luke asked.

"The inn's poltergeist. I promised him I'd pick up some fudge." I realized I was talking with my hands and promptly dropped them to my side.

"He can eat?"

"Er. No. It's a long story." I shook my head. "But I promised him I'd get it, trust me, you don't want to be on a poltergeist's bad side." I thought back to pranks Percy pulled in the past—the toad in my bed and the itching powder in my underwear were two of the worst that came to mind. I didn't want to think about what he'd do if I broke my word twice in one day.

"What kind?" Luke held the door open for me to walk in.

The moment I did, the sweet scent of chocolate hit me and my mouth watered. "Um. Just plain chocolate. That's his favorite."

"Okay, the one piece then?" Luke's question was innocent enough, but it felt like an attack on my will power.

I opened my mouth to say yes, but found myself saying, "And a couple pieces of rocky road, too." I couldn't help myself.

"Got it." Luke smiled that grin of his again, and I

promised that I would save mine until tomorrow, or after dinner at least.

Luke handed the bag over, and I met him at the register to pay. "Oh, I almost forgot. We're adding on a business decorating contest for this weekend. So, make sure you enter."

"Oh yeah?"

"Mm-hm. As long as the committee agrees. I'll have the forms ready in a bit. Stop by the registration desk?"

"Sounds good."

"Okay, great. Now I'm off. I'll see you later."

I said goodbye to Luke and the girls, who were hiding suspiciously outside behind a dogwood tree. I tried not to look over my shoulder as I walked past them, but man, it was hard not to. Like I said, those girls were trouble. You never knew what they were up to.

MIKE MCCORMICK WASN'T TOO hard to find. He was standing front and center on the stage, looking up at the placement of the lights, admiring his handiwork.

"It looks great, Mr. McCormick," I shouted up to him. Mike McCormick would forever be Mr. McCormick to me, no matter how many times he insisted I call him Mike. Growing up with his daughter Molly had meant he'd known me since before I could say my name, let alone write it. That placed him on a certain pedestal, like Mrs. Potts. Although, for the record, she never insisted I call her anything else.

Mr. McCormick had designed the stage as a rectangular prism on wheels. The face of the rectangle released on hinges, coming flat to form a stage. The top and back half of the rectangle was covered, creating the perfect alcove for a band, which we were fully taking advantage of. Miraculously, Witches Highway, a folk band with a fantastic fiddler who could stir the music within your soul, was available. It turned out the fiddler was fond of Silverlake, having vacationed in our enchanted town as a child and thus, sympathetic to our cause. I smiled at our good fortune.

"It'll do." Mr. McCormick was still looking up, hands on his hips. Satisfied, he cast his gaze down to me. "How're things on your end?"

"Ah, okay," I answered honestly. Starry Evans wasn't standing at the festival entrance anymore, but I knew she wasn't too far away, and soon, others would arrive. Not just reporters, those would come, as would Sophia's fans and regular folk full of morbid curiosity, too.

Mr. McCormick sensed my uneasiness. He took the stage's side steps and met me in the grass out front. "Terrible what happened to Sophia." He kept his voice low. "I heard you found her. You okay?"

"Yeah, I'll be okay. It was pretty awful, though." I tried to keep the images tucked away, but my brain cycled through them anyway. I was never one to volunteer to be magicked, but I might be willing to make an exception this time. Memory charms could be useful that way, or maybe Connie had a potion I could try in that new book of hers. For now, I shook the memories away like a polaroid picture. I cleared my throat and pressed on. "You knew her pretty well, didn't you?" If my memory served me right, Mr. McCormick graduated with Sophia. Same as my aunt and Arthur.

Mr. McCormick chuckled. "You could say that."

"There's a story there," I said with a smile, interpreting his comment.

"Isn't there always?" Mr. McCormick replied with laughter in his voice.

I politely waited for him to continue.

"Sophia and I were high school sweethearts." Mr. McCormick raised his eyebrows as if he couldn't believe it himself.

"I thought she dated Arthur in high school?" That's what Aunt Thelma said.

"Just the end of it. Prom to be exact." Mr. McCormick winced. It was funny how a memory all these years later could still cause you pain.

"I see." In a way, I could. I had gone to prom with Vance, and he ended up breaking my heart in the end anyway. Like grief, heartbreak stuck with you.

"It all worked out for the best. I hadn't wanted to move to California anyway." Mr. McCormick sounded genuine. It helped that I knew he adored his wife.

"Sophia was set on show biz right from the start, wasn't she?"

"Oh, she was, and I couldn't convince her otherwise, but then again, she couldn't convince me either. Werewolf blood," Mr. McCormick added by way of explanation.

"Hmm?"

"Made me impervious to her charms," Mr. McCormick tapped his fingertip to his temple. "Even though it's from a couple generations back." Come to think of it, now that I looked at him, his eyebrows were a bit bushier than the average man's. "And like I said, life worked out the way it was supposed to. If I would've married Sophia, I never would've met Betty and had Molly. So, as you can see, I have nothing to complain about. Well, except for my friendship with Arthur. That never did recover."

"If you and Arthur don't get along, then why did you guys go golfing yesterday?"

"What's that?"

"Arthur said he went golfing with you yesterday."

"Arthur?" Mr. McCormick looked incredulous.

"I'm positive. Actually, it was Sophia who'd said it."

"Sophia said I was golfing with Arthur?" Again Mr. McCormick repeated me.

His shock had me rethinking everything. I replayed the conversation in my head and nodded. "I'm sure of it."

"It beats me. I didn't even know Arthur was in town. I was too busy over here." Mr. McCormick motioned again to the grand stage behind him.

I changed the subject. "Thanks again for all your help."

"My pleasure. This festival's a good idea. Even if Mayor Parrish disagrees." Mr. McCormick lowered his voice at that last part.

"Yeah, she's not too happy with me." And that was before Sophia's death.

"Well, I, for one, am happy that you're back and the council agreed with you."

"Thanks Mr. McCormick." I blushed, not so much at Mr. McCormick's words, but because they made me think of Vance's similar praise from earlier.

"Call me Mike," the older man replied.

"Not a chance," I shot back with a smile and soon left, leaving Mr. McCormick to get back to work, and me, back to sleuthing.

CHAPTER TEN

I started to think that maybe Amber had been right taking Arthur in for questioning. His story didn't add up. He hadn't gone golfing with Mr. McCormick. I was one hundred percent convinced of that fact. Had Arthur even brought golf clubs home with him? I know some places allow you to rent them, but Arthur struck me as the type to prefer his own set, which meant he would've had to fly home with them, and I hadn't seen them at the inn. It was all adding up to more unanswered questions. More to the point, why lie? What had Arthur been up to, and did Sophia know about it?

Then there were Lorraine's comments. If the affair allegations were true, could Arthur have been meeting up with another woman? And again, if he wanted a believable alibi, why include Mr. McCormick?

I pondered the questions as I walked back to Mystic Inn. It would've been quicker to take the Enchanted Trail, but I still wasn't brave enough for that. No, I took the long way, walking along the side of the road, out in the open. This way, no one could jump out at me from the sloped lakeshore, and if any of the cars that drove by thought me odd, they didn't roll down their window and say so.

The parking lot at the inn was eerily empty, which wasn't a good sign. The place should have been bustling with activity—another ominous sign given the amount of work left to do. The only car left was Aunt Thelma's. I cautiously pushed the inn's glass-faced front door open and walked inside.

The lobby, like the parking lot, was deserted. I know we were technically closed to guests, but it was still unsettling to see the front desk unoccupied.

I surveyed the space, taking in the progress. Thankfully, the workmen had scraped up all the loose tile, leaving gray cement board behind. And Benny found a way to hang the new television above the mantel (hopefully with the correct bolt and spell). All the new lighting fixtures looked right, too. We couldn't have guests getting cracked in the head with falling lightbulbs, now could we. I could only imagine the online reviews if that had happened to a guest.

I walked around the counter, dropped off the bag of fudge, and glanced in the back office. Aunt Thelma never worked back there, but today was a day full of firsts, so I checked anyway.

But nope, no Aunt Thelma.

The afternoon sunlight poured through the lobby's full-length back windows. I walked over and looked through them onto the patio, but Aunt Thelma wasn't there either. Now that surprised me. The patio was one of her favorite spots, especially on sunny afternoons.

"Hmm." My thought escaped through my lips.

"Where's my fudge?" Percy's cool breath was unnaturally close to my ear. The proximity caused me to jump. My heart beat madly from the surprise. At least this time, I wasn't holding a cup of coffee to spill down the front of me.

"Will you quit doing that?" I hissed, turning on my heel to where Percy should've been standing, but he wasn't there.

"You promised!" Percy's disconnected voice said in my other ear. Again, his voice unnaturally close, almost as if he was inside my head. Goosebumps rose on my arms.

I swatted the air like you would an annoying fly. "It's over on the registration desk. Now, knock that off!"

Percy materialized. "Well...good then." Percy folded his arms across his chest.

"Any idea where Aunt Thelma is?" I took advantage of Percy's acceptance to change the subject.

"She's taking a nappy nap." Percy pointed up at the ceiling.

I looked up out of reflex. Percy took the opportunity to tug my ponytail.

Percy chuckled.

I opened my mouth to reply something witty, but once again, he was gone.

"Real mature!" I called out to the invisible poltergeist.

The candy shop bag magically floated off the counter.

"Hey, the rocky road fudge is mine, you hear? It's mine!" With my hands on my hips, I stared as the bag and invisible ghost continued down the hall.

"Not anymore," Percy's voice taunted in the distance.

I huffed a breath out my nose and tried to let it go. It was only fudge. I hadn't really *needed* it, anyway. But that doesn't mean I hadn't *wanted* it. Le-sigh.

Percy's laughter floated through the lobby as he retreated. I rolled my eyes, hoping he could see me, and then turned back to the window, exhaling and waiting for my heart rate to subside. As it did, I thought that a nap was probably just what Aunt Thelma needed. It had been a tough morning. I wouldn't be surprised in the least if she had sent the workmen on their way and decided to take a day off. Even with our crazy timeline, I couldn't fault her for it. And I sure wasn't about to go upstairs to the apartment and wake her either.

I turned back toward the lake, wondering what my next move should be when I spotted someone else that was a surprise.

Arthur was once again rowing a boat ashore.

I slid open the glass door and stepped onto the flag-stone patio. With my hand blocking the sun above my eyes, I watch Arthur as he smoothly dipped the paddles in and out of the water, gliding closer towards the inn.

The V-bottomed boat slid into the gravely sand with a satisfying crunch. Arthur pulled the oars in and stood, jumping down into the sand, pulling the boat the rest of the way onto the beach where we stored them during the day. He was barefoot, khaki pants rolled at the cuffs, wearing a button-down, short-sleeved shirt. I realized it was the same outfit he'd worn when Amber took him in for questioning a few hours ago.

Arthur still didn't realize I was watching him as he bent down and retrieved his loafers out of the bottom of the boat. With shoes in hand, he stood there, staring off across the lake. Shoulders dropping, he shook his head as if he was trying to come to terms with Sophia's death but still couldn't believe it.

My heart went out to the man. His posture certainly didn't look like someone who'd murdered his wife hours ago. No, he looked depressed, dejected—grief-stricken.

I cleared my throat, making my presence known. Arthur looked at me over his shoulder and then back across the lake. Kicking my shoes off, I left them on the patio and walked down the steps to the warm sand. The soft grains were pleasant this time of year, not burning like they would be in the summer, retaining heat for hours.

"You okay?" I asked when I joined Arthur's side, turning to read his expression.

Arthur bent low, dropping his shoes and plucking a rock from the shore. His thumb rubbed the smooth surface before flinging his wrist, causing the rock to skip across the lake. I watched as it danced across the surface, surprised at how far it made it before sinking below to the inky depths. I didn't think Arthur was going to answer my question, but then he said, "They think I killed Sophia."

I was going to deny it but decided it was best to go with the truth. "I know."

"Why?" This time Arthur did look to me. I realized it wasn't a rhetorical question. He honestly didn't understand why he was a suspect. I knew why I had my suspicions, but I wasn't sure what Amber was building her case on. Heck, she probably didn't even know.

"Where were you yesterday afternoon?"

Arthur visibly swallowed. He wasn't expecting me to ask that. "Looking at real estate." Arthur looked down with guilt.

I cocked my head, trying to make sense. "You guys were planning on moving back?" Or maybe Arthur meant a vacation home. I couldn't see Sophia leaving her California lifestyle, but I could see her agreeing to a southern vacation home. She probably would've filmed a cooking show or some other segment out of it. The setting fit her brand perfectly.

"Not us. Me." Arthur cleared his throat and left it at that. The meaning wasn't lost to me.

Oh. My mouth formed the word, but I didn't say it out loud. "Why did you say you were golfing with Mr. McCormick then?"

"I never said that. That was all Sophia. She thought she was funny," Arthur grunted at the memory. "Trying to remind me that another man had loved her, and I should consider myself lucky she chose me."

"Did you?"

"Hm?" Arthur seemed lost in his thoughts.

"Consider yourself lucky?"

Arthur shrugged. "I suppose I did, but not now. Now I don't know what I feel." Arthur picked up another rock and tossed it with too much force. It skated the surface of the water for a second, creating a wave as the lake swallowed it under.

"How long had it been like that?" I looked across the lake. My question was too personal for me to make eye contact. I would never have pried into his marriage if Lorraine's accusations weren't buzzing around in my brain like a hive full of angry bees.

"Oh, years." Arthur laughed without feeling. He put his hands on his hips and shook his head.

"And you stayed together because..." I let my words trail off, hoping Arthur would fill in the sentence.

"Because being married was good for her brand, and I was stupid enough to go along with it. I didn't realize or want to realize that she didn't, she couldn't—" Arthur shook his head, leaving his thoughts unspoken. They seemed too painful to finish.

I thought of Sophia's image—gorgeous house, doting husband, successful career—the perfect life. But it wasn't real because there's no such thing as a perfect life, no matter how hard we try to pretend otherwise.

We were silent for a moment. Across the lake, I spotted two older gentlemen out fishing. It was probably Roger and John. The older men were out on the lake every chance they could get when they weren't tending to the flower shop or driving a cab, respectively.

"Some things never change," Arthur motioned to the men fishing.

"No, I guess they don't."

We dropped back to silence. The boat slipped on by, fishing lines out on either side.

Finally, I said. "Lorraine. She said some things."

"Oh, I bet she did," Arthur said in a clipped voice.

"Forgive me for asking, but it might explain why you're a suspect." I cleared my throat, uncomfortable with what I was about to ask.

Arthur looked at me expectantly.

I hesitated. "Were there other women?"

"Ha, it would've been better if there were," Arthur bit back. "I was one hundred percent faithful to Sophia. Followed her around like a puppy dog." Arthur seemed disgusted with himself.

"Why would Lorraine say that then?"

Arthur raked his fingers through his hair in agitation. "Lorraine's never liked me, never thought I was good enough. She wanted to manage a power couple. Tried to fill Sophia's head with lies, convince her to leave me."

"Did Sophia believe her?"

"Never. Sophia had her ways. People can say what they want, but Sophia was a powerful witch. Besides, Sophia didn't want a husband that was her equal, believe me." I wasn't sure what Arthur meant by that, but he didn't give me a chance to ask because he kept right on talking, "But she never stopped Lorraine from running her mouth, either." Again, Arthur stared across the lake. "I can't believe she was right," Arthur muttered.

"Who was right?"

Arthur sighed. It was the sound of someone weary of the world. "I'm sorry, but I need a minute," his voice was a mere whisper.

I took a step back. "I understand. Listen, before I leave, I just want to say that I'm sorry for your loss."

"Thank you," Arthur nodded, looking down.

"I also want to say that I don't think Deputy Reynolds is going to leave you alone. It might be smart if you got a lawyer."

"I know," Arthur said on a sigh. He didn't look too happy with the prospect, but he was smart enough to know I was right.

"If you're looking for someone, I recommend Vance Blackwell. He's a friend of mine," I said by way of explanation.

"Boyd Andrews still practicing?" Arthur looked up, caught my eye.

Boyd should've retired years ago, but he was still practicing law, as I suspected he would until the day he died.

"Or you could give Boyd a call," I agreed.

"But you'd call Vance," Arthur surmised.

"I would," and that was the truth. Regardless of my

past with Vance, I'd trust him any day, especially when it came to the law.

"Thanks. I'll look into him," Arthur turned back to the lake and zoned out.

Realizing our conversation was over, I said, "I'll be inside if you need anything," and left Arthur to his thoughts.

"What did he have to say?" Aunt Thelma asked from behind the front desk.

"You're up," I said by way of greeting.

"And I feel better for resting." Aunt Thelma patted her pinned back red hair as if making sure it was all in place. It was, of course. Aunt Thelma didn't need bobby pins or hairspray for the task either. Only her wand.

"Well, I'm glad to hear it."

"How's Arthur?" Aunt Thelma looked over my shoulder to where Arthur was still standing outside.

"I'm not sure." I couldn't think of a single word to describe Arthur. It required several.

"What did he say?" Aunt Thelma asked again.

"That he was Sophia's lapdog, and Lorraine hates his guts." I summarized it as best as I could.

"Huh."

I couldn't read Aunt Thelma's non-committal remark. "What does that mean?"

"Just that I suppose that I'm not surprised, and perhaps, I can relate," Aunt Thelma added after a pause. Her eyebrows raised at the end of the statement.

"I suggested he call Vance. Knowing Amber, she'll

zero in on him and prosecute him despite a lack of hard evidence."

"You don't think he did it," Aunt Thelma remarked.

"I don't. Despite how convenient it would be otherwise. But it does make me wonder about Lorraine."

"Speak of the devil," Aunt Thelma muttered.

Lorraine sashayed into the lobby and abruptly stopped when she spotted Arthur. "They let him out?" she said more to herself than anybody. She scoffed, ignoring us, and marched straight out the back door and down the steps to lay into him.

We watched as she pointed her finger in Arthur's face, accusations flying.

Arthur stood there, letting Lorraine tear into him. Her arms waved about. It went on for a few minutes. Lorraine's voice rose in volume and pitch as the seconds ticked by. Eventually, her shrieking reached our ears inside.

I winced. It was like watching a train wreck. You couldn't look away even though you should.

But when Lorraine pushed Arthur's shoulder, sending him stumbling backward, Aunt Thelma had had enough, which was exactly what she said.

"Enough." Aunt Thelma pulled her wand out with a huff and walked over to the door.

I held my breath, not sure what my aunt was about to do.

Opening the door, Aunt Thelma pointed the wand at Lorraine and said "berdévo," temporarily befuddling the woman.

"Aunt Thelma!" I hissed, rushing over to see the after-effects, praying the woman was still in one piece.

Lorraine's mouth snapped shut, and she looked up to the sky as if it held the answers to her current confusion. Hands on her hips, she then looked from side to side, trying to make sense of it all before settling back up to the sky.

I had to admit, the silence was a welcome respite.

Arthur looked over at where we stood, and catching Aunt Thelma's eye, he smiled. It was the first time I'd seen the man genuinely smile. His grin was broad, and he looked ten years younger, if not more.

Aunt Thelma waved from the door.

I shook my head, but I couldn't bring myself to chastise my aunt. It was a smart move, even if I wasn't willing to admit it.

"What?" Aunt Thelma looked back at me innocently. "She deserved it."

I didn't disagree.

Aunt Thelma walked back to the front desk. "Now, what were you saying?"

I couldn't even remember. "I think it was about Lorraine?"

"Oh yes, right. Do you think she has a motive?"

"Not that I know of. But even if she did, she didn't get in until today." Lorraine could've called and threatened Sophia from anywhere, but she would've had to have been here to kill her.

"So, she said," Aunt Thelma motioned to Lorraine's

bags behind the counter. The airline tags were still on them.

I walked around the counter and inspected them, surprised at what I found. "She got in last night?"

"Five o'clock flight from Atlanta."

"Giving her plenty of time drive here and kill Sophia. I'm calling Vance." If he did end up representing Arthur, he needed to know everything. "But wait," I groaned. "I don't have a phone."

"Where's your phone?" Aunt Thelma looked behind me as if my phone was smashed on the ground.

"It went for a swim this morning. I need to file a claim." Which meant I needed to jump online and see if there was a way to do it on the computer, or if I could find a number to call from the inn's landline.

Aunt Thelma shook her head. "You're still thinking like a mortal."

I cocked my head, "What's that supposed to mean?" I tried not to get defensive, but it was hard. I wished I was more witchy than I was.

Aunt Thelma ignored my question. "Just order a new one from Witch-Mart. Pay for it online, and conjure it in seconds."

"What? That's a thing?"

"If you know what you're doing." Aunt Thelma shrugged like it was no big deal.

"Um, maybe you better do it?" It might end up in Biloxi with the inn's furniture if I gave it a try. "I'll get my debit card."

CHAPTER ELEVEN

F ifteen minutes later, I called Vance on my new phone on my way out the door.

"Angelica?" Aunt Thelma called behind me. I stopped with one hand on the door and the other one holding my phone to my ear. I turned around. Aunt Thelma met me and handed me her car keys.

"It will be quicker," she said.

"Thanks."

"What's that?" Vance asked me when our lines connected.

"Nothing, I was just talking to my aunt. Are you free right now?"

I could hear papers rustling on the other end of the line.

"Yeah, just finishing up."

"How'd it go?"

"Good. Jury found her innocent, so..." Vance didn't

finish the sentence. I could picture him shrugging on the other end of the line.

"Congrats."

"Thank you. So, what's going on? I see you got your new phone."

"Did you know you can conjure them?"

"I did. Guess I should've told you that."

"Not your fault. Anyway, I have loads to tell you. Want to meet me at the taco truck?" Silverlake's latest restaurant wasn't tied to a location at all, but you could almost always find it across from the high school on weekdays. It was a perfect location as teenagers always seemed to have the largest appetite and extra money to spend. If not, the business district was a short walk away, giving townsfolk an excuse to take a walk on their lunch hour. It was a win-win for everyone.

Fifteen minutes later, I parked Aunt Thelma's car against the curb. I spotted Vance standing off to the side of the food truck and talking on his cell phone. I waited in the car for a couple minutes, giving him time to wrap up his conversation before getting out to meet him.

"Sounds good... I will for sure be in touch ... You too...Bye."

"Hey, how's it going?" I said once Vance turned his attention toward me.

"Good. That was Arthur. Thanks for the recommendation. He went ahead and asked me to represent him." Vance slipped the phone back into his back pocket.

"Good, that's a smart move. I think Amber's going to martyr him."

"It wouldn't be the first time."

"Isn't that the truth."

"How'd it go with Rick?"

"That's what I wanted to talk to you about."

Together we moved to get in line for our lunch. We weren't the only people craving the street fare. It looked like the whole football team was in line ahead of us. I was careful to keep my voice low.

"Misty and I met up with Rick's wife, Kayla."

"Sophia's niece."

"Yes." I tucked a wayward strand of hair behind my ear. "She hadn't yet heard about Sophia."

"A bit surprising, but not all that unusual, seeing it happened this morning."

"I'll give you that, but Rick came home while we were there."

Something about my expression gave my thoughts away.

"And he knew," Vance finished my sentence.

"He did, and he wasn't very happy to see us."

Vance raised his eyebrows. "I bet. What did he say about getting into it with Sophia?"

"Kayla didn't know about that either, but Rick didn't deny it when Misty brought it up. In Rick's defense, he said it was because he came home yesterday and Kayla was upset because of Sophia."

"He felt it was his place to put Sophia in hers." Vance surmised.

"Right." I tucked my sweater tighter across my chest and folded my arms to keep it in place. The air had turned cooler than I had expected today. Vance and I took a moment to look over the daily specials written on the whiteboard outside the truck. The hot pink and lime green script advertised pulled pork or Korean beef, two of my favs, plus the regular chicken and fish tacos, which were also excellent.

"Tough decision," Vance mumbled.

"Mmm-hmm." It was going to be.

"Did Rick say why Kayla was upset with Sophia?" Vance asked after a moment.

"Hmm?" I turned from the menu and gave Vance my full attention.

Vance repeated the question.

"No, he didn't. And Kayla didn't say anything about it either. I'm sure one of us would've asked if Rick hadn't thrown us out after that."

"He threw you out?" Vance's expression turned dark. His hand balled into a fist at his side.

"Metaphorically speaking." I kept the rest of the details vague. "Anyway, I'm not worried about him. He clearly doesn't have anything to hide."

Again, we moved up in line.

"Okay, so if it's not Rick, and you don't think it's Arthur, who do you think it is?"

"How do you know I don't think it's Arthur?"

Vance gave me a look that said, "*Are you serious?*" But out loud he said, "Because you referred him to me?"

"Okay, fair point."

Vance smiled, looking every inch a dashing Prince Charming.

No, I shook my head.

Vance was not Prince Charming. I needed to put a stop to romantic notions of my ex.

"Are you okay?" Vance asked.

"What? Yeah, I'm fine. Just hungry. What are you getting?"

"It's a toss-up between the pulled pork and Korean BBQ."

"Same." Now it was my turn to smile.

Our conversation was on hold until after we ordered and got our food. There were just too many people standing around for us to talk comfortably.

Finally, with our paper baskets full of tacos and strawberry lemonade in hand, Vance and I found an empty park bench and sat down. It would be a few more minutes before our conversation drifted back to talking about the case. It turned out I was hungry.

"So, not Rick or Arthur," Vance said.

I nodded my head and swallowed. Taking another sip of my drink, I said, "No, but I'm thinking Lorraine."

"You didn't like her from the moment you met her." Vance took another bite of taco, holding it over his basket as the spicy mayo dripped out. Tacos could be a bit messy, but they were worth it.

"No, I didn't. But that's not why. Remember Lorraine said she'd just gotten in?"

"She lied?"

"Mm-hmm. Aunt Thelma pointed out her baggage claim tags. She flew in last night."

"Why lie if she's not hiding something?"

"My point exactly." It was my turn to try the Korean taco. I closed my eyes and sighed as I chewed. The beef, kimchi, and spicy mayo combination was just as good as last time. Talk about culinary perfection.

Vance ignored my food nirvana and pressed on. "Okay, so we need to look into Lorraine. Run a background check, public record search, insurance policies, the works."

"You mean we need to find a motive."

Vance continued eating while I sipped on my drink and thought.

"What about how Sophia died?"

"What about it?" Vance asked.

"You'd have to be pretty strong to drown someone. I suppose the murderer could've killed her first and then disposed of her in the lake." I shivered, and it had nothing to do with the weather or the icy beverage I held.

"You're thinking like a mortal." Vance wiped his mouth with a napkin.

"You're the second person to tell me that today." I scowled.

"Sorry."

I waved Vance's comment away and encouraged him to continue by saying, "You think someone killed her with a spell?"

"Possibly, or another supernatural could've been involved."

"You mean like a shifter?" I thought back to how easily Dr. Humphrey had pulled Sophia's body out of the lake.

"Right."

"Sophia did have a bit to drink last night. Not sure if that came into play." I thought back to the empty bottles of wine. Sophia drank three glasses to my one.

"Maybe she drank poison or a potion."

I thought for a moment. "I don't know. We all drank from the same wine bottle. But I guess we can't rule that out. I mostly thought that if she were tipsy, it would've made it easier to sneak up on her."

"Did Arthur keep refilling her glass?"

I tipped my head to the side while I thought and remembered that Sophia kept reaching for the bottle, and I said as much. "But she didn't seem drunk. I have no idea how she ended the night, though."

"So, we have a slightly tipsy Sophia, at a minimum."

"And a killer supernatural who possibly took advantage of the situation."

"That widens the suspect pool a bit." Silverlake was known as a safe haven for witches, but a fair share of other supernaturals called our town home. Except for vampires. They kept to themselves. A fact for which I was thankful. I shivered again.

"You want to get going?" Vance asked, misinterpreting my chill.

"No, I'm okay. Just thinking about murder and

vampires," I mumbled the last part, but Vance still heard me.

"Vampires?" Vance raised a quizzical brow.

"Nothing, never mind." I blushed despite my best efforts not to.

Thankfully, Vance dropped it and instead said, "You said someone called and threatened Sophia last night, right?"

"Yeah, during dinner." I tried to recall the conversation. "Sophia told them to back off and stop threatening her, or something like that." I couldn't remember her exact words.

"We'll need to check her phone records then too."

"Amber is never going to give us that information."

"No, but she'll give it to Arthur's attorney."

I opened my mouth, ready to retort, but smiled instead. "That's brilliant."

"And it also happens to be true, especially if Amber charges Arthur with murder, which could happen any minute if my sources are correct."

"Oh man, poor Arthur." I looked down at the rest of my lunch. I suddenly wasn't feeling very hungry anymore.

"Shall we?" Vance stood.

I copied the motion but had a different plan in mind.

CHAPTER TWELVE

W e agreed to meet at Vance's office in an hour. I wanted to go back to the inn and draft up the contest entry form before this afternoon's festival meeting at Clemmie's tea shop. I also figured Vance would have better luck at the sheriff's department without me present. While I appreciated his offer to accompany him, I knew it wasn't a smart move. Amber might have to make Vance privy to the information, but she sure didn't have to share anything with me. And I knew she'd fight broom and wand to keep it that way.

This time, I wasn't surprised to see the front desk deserted. Percy wasn't anywhere in sight either. About the only thing that was where it was when I left was Lorraine's fancy-schmancy luggage. No way was she leaving town without it. I took out my cell phone, and took a picture of her luggage tags in case it turned out to be evidence. I didn't need Lorraine to realize her mistake and destroy them, making it her word against mine (because, let's be honest, we all know how that would go down.)

I tucked my cell phone back in my pocket and walked back to the office, ready to create the layout for the entry form.

But it turned out the form was going to have to wait.

Opening my laptop, I found a note. I recognized Aunt Thelma's handwriting before reading a single word. This couldn't be good. Dread washed over me. Instinctively, I reached for the tiger's eye around my neck as if the pendant could stop whatever Aunt Thelma had put into motion.

I'm taking a little trip with Arthur. Don't worry, dear. We're fine. We're going to let this mess blow over. I'm sure you understand.

Love,

Aunt Thelma

P.S.

Everything will work out with the inn. You'll see.

"She left?" I reread the note, still in shock that my aunt would up and run away with Arthur. "What is she thinking?" It was a rhetorical question. I knew what she was thinking. She didn't want Arthur to go through what she did last month. If anyone knew what it was like to be falsely accused, it was Aunt Thelma. But then the devil on my shoulder started talking.

What if Arthur wasn't innocent?

What if he killed Sophia?

What if my aunt was galivanting off to who knows where with a madman?

I began pacing the small space.

"Ooh, Jelly's mad." Percy appeared in the doorway, his prized fudge in his hand.

"Shush. Up." I bit back at the ghost before finding my manners. "Sorry, not mad at you. Just worried about Aunt Thelma." I heaved a sigh and took in the poltergeist for the first time. Percy had slicked back his white hair and donned a brown tweed sports coat, topping the look off with a red striped bowtie. I was pretty sure my ex-boyfriend, Allen, had the same outfit. In fact, I was sure of it, which made me question that relationship for the hundredth time.

I cautiously sniffed the air. "Is that cologne?" I moved one step closer, and I fanned the air in front of my face. My eyes started to water. It was a lot of cologne.

If a ghost could blush, Percy would've.

"What are you up to?" I cocked my head to the side, trying to read the poltergeist.

"N-n-n-nothing," Percy stammered, folding his arms across his chest, clutching the fudge in the process.

"Do you have a date?"

"It's not a date!"

I ducked just in time as a box of staples flew past me. The small package skidded across the desk and onto the floor. Hence the poltergeist part of Percy's name.

I would've pushed it further, but I didn't want

Percy to chuck the stapler next. As it was, I had other pressing matters on my hands other than Percy's social life.

"Okay, not a date. But before you go wherever it is you're going, can you tell me if you saw Aunt Thelma leave?"

"You betcha." Percy rocked back on his heels.

"With Arthur," I clarified.

"Uh-huh." Percy rolled back down on his toes.

"And you didn't try and stop them?" The pitch of my voice ratcheted up a notch.

Percy shook his head. "You know what your problem is, Jelly?"

Oh, boy. Here we go. I crossed my arms like a petulant child for a moment before realizing how ridiculous I looked and thrust my hands in my pockets instead. What could I say? Percy brought out the six-year-old in me.

Percy didn't wait for me to respond. "You need to lighten up."

"Is that so?" I gave the poltergeist a steely glare.

"Always complaining." Percy furrowed his brow and started stomping around the office. "It's never going to be done in time. It's a disaster! Aunt Thelma, what are we going to do?" Percy threw his arms up in the air, mocking me.

"I do not sound like that." I was back to folding my arms across my chest defiantly.

Percy stopped parading around and stared at me.

"Sure, and I'm not a poltergeist." His words dripped with sarcasm.

I deflated a bit. "Okay, point taken. But I am worried about Aunt Thelma. What if Arthur's a killer?"

"He's not." Percy looked down and examined his fingernails as if he hadn't a care in the world. Or maybe he really didn't have a care in the world. It was hard to say. I mean, how much could a ghost have to worry about?

"How do you know?"

"I don't know. I just do. Now, if you don't mind, I have someplace to be. Not a date," Percy quickly added before disappearing.

"It's totally a date." My voice was barely audible.

"It's not," Percy replied in a sing-songy voice from somewhere unknown.

"Whatever you say," I said on an exhale.

I looked back down at the note and hoped Aunt Thelma and Percy were right.

And then I called the only other person I could think of.

"Hey," I said when Vance answered the phone.

"Sorry, it's taking a bit longer down here. Amber isn't cooperating." Vance's voice sounded strained.

That wasn't surprising. Amber never cooperated, but in this case, it didn't make much sense. "Why not?"

"Because Arthur hasn't been formally charged."

"And you're on a need-to-know basis?" I surmised.

"You got it. Unless they charge him, I can't access Sophia's phone records."

Talk about a catch-22. Luckily, or maybe it was unluckily, I might be able to help. "About that." I let my voice trail off.

"What, what's happened?" Vance jumped on my words like a dog with a bone.

"Aunt Thelma and Arthur have run away." I blurted the words out and closed my eyes, still unable to believe it myself.

"What? Are you sure?"

"I have the note right here." I glanced back at the paper beside my computer.

"Excuse me," Vance said to someone on his end of the line. I could tell he was on the move. "I'll be there in ten minutes."

We said our goodbyes, and then I fired off a group text, asking the festival committee if we could meet tomorrow morning at Clemmie's shop, Sit For a Spell, instead. Clemmie replied that ten o'clock would work best, and we all agreed to meet then. I hated putting the meeting off, but solving this case was too important. It's funny how twenty-four hours could completely alter one's priorities.

A second later, Misty texted me. "Is everything okay?"

I weighed my response before messaging back, "Yeah. I'll call you later?"

"I'm out at eight," Misty replied.

I messaged back a thumbs up and tucked my phone away, trying not to feel guilty for leaving Misty out of the loop. Bless my best friend, but Misty had a mouth on her. She wouldn't tell anyone on purpose, but she'd let it slip, and then all of Silverlake would know. I didn't want word to get out, not until I talked to Vance.

Speaking of which, he made it to me in seven minutes.

"So, what's going on?" Vance walked straight into the office and sat across the desk from me.

I handed him the note.

His eyes scanned the paper. "I can't believe it." We're the first words out of his mouth.

"Me either." We made eye contact as the gravity of the situation settled between us.

"This could speed up the arraignment. Did you tell anyone else?"

"Just Percy, but he was here when they left. What should we do?"

"Do you want the sheriff to find them?"

I hesitated before realizing the truth. "I don't think he can. Aunt Thelma's a powerful witch. If she's in the wind, the sheriff won't find her unless she wants him to."

"That's a good point."

"And," I continued on a roll, "I suppose that should make me feel better, too. Aunt Thelma can hold her own." As much as I liked to give my aunt grief, she was good with the wand, especially charm work. She could protect herself if it came down to that.

"Also true. But it does make Arthur look suspicious. The innocent don't run."

I visibly swallowed. My mouth was suddenly dry. I

looked around the office, but I hadn't left a water bottle on or near the desk like usual. Instead, I cleared my throat and said, "Do you have to tell the sheriff?" I wasn't sure what the law was here.

"No, but we can. He was already planning on charging Arthur. Like I said, this news might speed up the process."

"Do you know what evidence they have?" Again, I was pretty sure Arthur was innocent but not one hundred percent convinced. I'd feel better knowing it was all circumstantial.

"Not yet. It's Amber's case, and she's not letting Jones talk."

I puffed out my cheeks in frustration. Deputy Jones was a good guy. If we could talk to him alone, he'd probably help us out. Maybe not turn over Sophia's phone records, but he'd tell us what they had on Arthur. I pictured Arthur standing dejected at the water's edge. Either he was a great actor, or he was innocent.

I weighed my options and decided to trust my aunt. "Let's give it until tomorrow and see what we can discover tonight." I might come to regret my decision, but at that moment, it felt right.

Vance nodded. "Okay."

I loved that he didn't question my decision or try and talk me out of it.

"Let me grab my bag, and we'll get to work." Vance walked out the office door.

I nodded and stood, walking out the door after him

to grab two bottles of water, a pack of cookies, and put on the coffee pot. Something told me it was going to be a long night.

Vance got to work, starting with Lorraine. Within minutes he ordered the background check and ran a public records search.

Vance whistled, turning his computer to face me. "This is going to take a while."

"What's all that?" I leaned forward and squinted at the screen. Several rows of text stared back.

"Lorraine's public record. We've got parking tickets, divorce records—a couple of those—an assault charge. Wait, make that two assault charges."

"What?" I turned Vance's computer back around.

Vance pointed at the screen. "Alex Blanco filed two assault charges last year."

I thought for a moment. "Is he one of her exes?"

"Good idea. Hang on. Let me check the divorce record." Vance turned the computer back toward him. His fingers clicked on the keyboard and then waited, presumably for the next screen to load. I watched his eyes scan the screen. "And...yes. They divorced about six months ago."

"Can you get a number for him?" If Lorraine had a history of violence, I wanted to know all about it. Prior records would help build Lorraine's character profile.

"Probably. Hang on."

I left Vance to track down the number and turned back to my computer. I was digging deeper into

Sophia's past. Silverlake Chronicle had done a decent job keeping track of her success over the years. Of course, so did Witch News Network, but I was back to operating under the assumption that whoever killed Sophia was a local (if not Lorraine). I scrolled through the Chronicle's press releases and accompanying pictures, looking to see if anything popped out.

"Do you remember this?" It was my turn to share my computer screen with Vance. The article was from a fall pie competition about ten years ago. The black and white picture showed a beaming Sophia. Aunt Thelma stood beside her, awarding her the first place ribbon. Diane stood off to the side. She wasn't glaring per se, but she wasn't smiling either.

Vance looked over. "No. I was living in Florida then."

"Diane said she stole her pie recipe. Wonder if this was when she found out." I pointed to Diane's scowl.

Vance looked closer at the picture. "Could be. Are you suggesting Diane killed Sophia over pie?"

I breathed out my nose. "I don't know what I'm suggesting." I sat with my thoughts for a moment. "Maybe not Diane, but if Sophia was willing to swindle a friend, then who knows who else has it out for her?"

"The list could be long."

"Indeed."

Vance and I worked in companionable silence. Our fingers tapped away on our keyboards as we continued our deep dive.

"Forget that list of yours." Vance's voice interrupted the quiet.

"What'd you find?" I looked up. Vance's eyes gleamed with excitement.

Vance swiveled his computer around to me and stood, walking around to join me on my side of the desk. Bending low, over my shoulder, he pointed at his screen.

I read through the document, trying to ignore the pine and sage scent that clung to Vance and filled my senses, but it was mighty difficult. "What am I looking at?" It was an insurance document, that much I could tell, but it wasn't life insurance.

"Lorraine had key man insurance on Sophia."

The revolution meant more to Vance than it did me. "What's that?"

"Think of it as life insurance for a key person in a business. Like a company might insure its CEO. A restauranteur, his chef."

Catching on, I interrupted, "Or a business manager, her star client."

"Exactly. And Lorraine went big with a million-dollar policy." Vance read through the details on the screen.

"So instead of losing Sophia as a client, Lorraine could've killed her and cashed out."

"Right. Wonder how their relationship was?"

"Sophia was thinking of leaving the business." I lifted my index finger to make my point.

"What?" Vance stood, no longer lingering over my

shoulder. Not that I complained about his close proximity. Heaven help me.

"Didn't I tell you that?" I turned in my chair so that we were facing one another.

"No. You didn't."

"She was thinking of it. That's what Aunt Thelma said at dinner. Although Arthur was skeptical Sophia would follow through."

"But if Lorraine thought it was possible..."

"She might have acted before it was too late." I finished Vance's sentence.

"Looks like we found our motive."

"So, Lorraine lies, flies in last night. Calls and threatens Sophia during dinner. Sophia agrees to meet up with her later, and then what? Lorraine drowns her in the lake?"

"Or curses her and disposes of the body in the lake. Something like that."

"Lorraine's a supernatural of some sort. I assumed she was a witch, but she could be a shifter too."

Vance and I stared at one another for a moment.

"Do you want to call it in, or should I?" he asked.

"You, definitely you. You don't by chance have a direct line to Deputy Jones, do you?"

"Already there." Vance had his phone out and was dialing the deputy's number.

I listened to the conversation as it unfolded.

"Hey Jones, I've uncovered something you might want to know."

Vance took a minute to relay the information. From

my end, it sounded like Deputy Jones was interested, and who wouldn't be? We delivered opportunity and motive right to his desk. Now all he had to do was find some evidence to back it up, and it would be a closed case.

CHAPTER THIRTEEN

I was so wrapped up in Vance's conversation that I almost didn't hear the person out front.

Stepping away from Vance, I walked over to the doorjamb and peered out front just in time to see Lorraine wheel her luggage toward the front door.

"Lorraine!" I shouted, throwing a panicked look over my shoulder.

I didn't wait for Vance to follow me as I bolted after her, thankful loose tiles no longer littered the floor.

Lorraine had a cab waiting out front. She tossed her bag in unceremoniously, ready to jump in the backseat and take off when I reached her.

"Lorraine, wait!" I held my hand out to stop her.

Lorraine was already inside the car. Her arm ready to yank the car door shut. "I can't. I have to go. I have a flight to catch, sorry." Her voice sounded anything but apologetic.

Vance caught up with us at that moment. His phone was still to his ear.

"If you'll excuse me." Lorraine wasn't waiting for us to say goodbye.

If I didn't act fast, Lorraine would be gone, and we might never solve the case. Thinking quickly, I pulled out my wand and shouted, "Stasi!" to stun Lorraine. Or that's what I meant to say, but clearly that's not what came out. A flash of purple light shot out of my wand, and in the next minute, Lorraine was transformed into a sloth.

Vance snorted behind me.

My mouth dropped.

"What's up with you and the animals?" Vance asked between laughs.

I groaned. "I was just trying to stop her!"

"Obviously." Vance was still laughing behind me. He was, however, no longer on the phone.

The cab driver and long-time resident, John Delroe, snickered. "I wasn't about to drive off, Miss Nightingale."

"Now you tell me," I sighed, shaking my head at John.

Lorraine looked up at me from the backseat and blinked in slow motion. I had no idea how much of her personality remained in the animal, and I wasn't eager to find out.

I looked down at the slim piece of wood in my hand. That's what I got for carrying a wand with dragon heartstring for its core. Well, that and unicorn hair. But it was the heartstring that gave the wand its transfiguration power. And why Lorraine was now covered in fur, and I was wondering what to do next.

As if reading my mind, Vance said, "Deputy Jones is on his way."

I looked up. I wasn't sure that was a good thing or not. If Amber was with him, she was bound to charge me with unlawful transfiguration.

I eyed Lorraine skeptically, or make that her rather long nails. I never realized just how long sloth finger-nails grew. I also realized that I knew next to nothing about sloths and their defense mechanisms.

Vance must've sensed my hesitation. He stepped forward and scooped Lorraine up. She gladly wrapped her arms around his neck and held on like a monkey, or make that a sloth. Vance walked back toward the inn.

"Right." I turned back to John. "Mind unloading Lorraine's luggage?"

"No problem." John put the car into park and got out. "I'll just put them inside."

"Thanks, John."

I trailed after Vance and followed him back into the office. He carefully deposited Lorraine on the chair in front of my desk. She sat there with her legs crossed and her arms folded casually in her lap. If Lorraine was agitated, she didn't look it. Or maybe sloths just always looked easygoing. It was hard to tell.

I looked away and refocused on the problem at hand.

"Okay, here's what I'm thinking," I said as I paced

the office. "We wait until Deputy Jones pulls in, and then you reverse the spell. If Lorraine runs, we'll let Deputy Jones tackle her. If she sits put, at least she'll be human, and I won't get in trouble for transfiguring her. Sound good?"

Vance barely had time to nod his ascent before the deputy's cruiser pulled in the parking lot.

"Oh, they're here already?" I shot a nervous look at Vance. Deputy Jones hadn't come alone. I spotted Amber in the front seat, looking smug as ever. My palms turned sweaty, and I prayed this would all work out okay.

Vance waited for a beat, and then pointing his wand at Lorraine, said, "Adikos," to reverse the previous spell.

In a blink, Lorraine roared back to life, and I mean roared. "You cursed me! Did anyone else see that! How dare you! I'm pressing charges." Lorraine got all huffy. Her face reddened, and she looked like she was going to strangle me.

I backed up until the back of my thighs hit the table behind me. My hands braced the table for support.

Lorraine looked to Vance to back her up, but she was on her own. Vance shook his head as if he had no idea what Lorraine was talking about. I tried to look innocent, but Lorraine wasn't buying it. Clearly, her memory was intact.

"You'll pay for this. Why I ought to take care of you both right now." Lorraine's eyes glowed, the irises turning a dark amber color. She stalked forward, the way a lion hunts its prey.

My mouth went dry. I glanced nervously over at Vance, who seemed too stunned to move. We both were. Where in the world were the deputies? What was taking them so long?

I looked down at Lorraine's hands. Paws had replaced her fingers—large paws with razor-sharp claws and spotted fur. Lorraine wasn't a lion. She was a leopard.

Holy cats. It wouldn't do me a lick of good to transform into my feline alter ego. Once Lorraine had completely transformed, she would hunt me down in a flash, and that would be the end of me. No, I was better off staying in human form.

Lorraine slashed at the air.

I sucked in my breath. Leaning back against the table, the wood cut into my back.

Lorraine's nail snagged my sweater, ripping right through it. Later I'd think about how she had ruined my favorite gray sweater, but right then, I was just thankful it wasn't my spleen.

Vance came to his senses. "Elaxei!" The words flew out of his mouth in a flash, the memory charm hitting Lorraine in the back. Vance held his wand in place, speaking slow and clear, planting an alternative memory in its place. "You came here to get your luggage but found out that Deputy Jones wants to talk to you. He'll be here any second. Have a seat."

In a trance, Lorraine took a step back and then

another. Her hands returned to her human state, and she slowly made her way over to the chair.

"That's it now," Vance coaxed Lorraine.

Lorraine nodded numbly and plopped down in the chair. Her eyes held a far-off gaze about them.

"Everything is okay. Just answer the deputy's questions, and then you can go." Vance lowered his wand.

Lorraine nodded.

I stood shaking, off to the side, trying to look composed but failing miserably.

"Desperate times call for desperate measures," Vance said under his breath to me. "You okay?" He turned to me, his eyes assessing my appearance.

"Yeah, I'm fine."

"Good," Vance replied, even though we both knew that I was lying.

"Hello?" Deputy Jones called from out front.

"Back here." Vance looked at me with concern in his eyes before clearing his expression, replacing it with something more passive.

I tried to do the same, plastering a fake smile on my face and folding my hands in front of me, hoping the deputies didn't realize they were still shaking.

"Your sweater," Vance whispered.

I looked down. I wasn't a slave to fashion, but this wouldn't do. At the last minute, I tugged my sweater over my head and tied it around my waist, thankful for the tanktop underneath. It was a little cool for the look but easier than explaining the torn sweater.

"'This is a waste of time," Amber said, joining her partner as they entered the office.

Amber meant the comment for her partner, but that didn't stop me from responding. "I don't think so. You should hear what we have to say," My voice held a matter-of-fact tone. I was proud of how calm I sounded.

"Well, let's hear it then." Amber was annoyed with me. At this point, I was used to it.

I nodded to Vance to take the lead. I didn't trust my voice not to break. The adrenaline rush was wearing off, and I was worried my knees would go weak any minute. I casually sat down at my desk opposite Lorraine. For her part, she looked like she had no idea how she came to be where she was. It looked like Vance's spell had worked, and that was just fine with me. If she could forget that I transfigured her, then I could forget she attacked me, especially if she was going down for murder.

"We found a key man policy in Lorraine's name for Sophia to the tune of a million dollars."

"Is that so?" Deputy Jones looked to Lorraine to deny it, but instead, she sat there quietly, staring off a bit. I wasn't sure if it was the after-effects of the memory charm or if she really didn't have anything to say.

"But Lorraine wasn't in town last night," Amber stated like the rest of us were a bunch of idiots.

"Actually, she was." I stepped out and found Lorraine's luggage, wheeling it back to the office as evidence. The deputies turned their attention my way.

"Her baggage tags are still attached. She got in last night."

"And she's a leopard shifter. Plenty strong enough to do the job," Vance added.

That seemed to snap Lorraine out of it. She closed her eyes and put her fingertips on her temples as if she couldn't believe this was happening. Then she stood, as if that somehow gave her an advantage. I couldn't help it. I backed up against the back table again. My eyes darted down to my wand. I'd rather turn her into a sloth than have her pounce on me once more.

"Stop. Stop all of this. You have it all wrong." Lorraine placed her hands on the desk before her.

Lorraine caught my eye. I raised my eyebrows in response, not believing her for a second. From the looks on Vance's and Deputy Jones' faces, they didn't believe her either. Amber was the only one giving Lorraine the benefit of the doubt.

"I did get in last night. But I wasn't in Silverlake. I stayed in Atlanta. Here." Lorraine dug her cell phone out of her pocket and pulled up her hotel reservation on her phone. "You can call the hotel. They'll confirm I was there."

"That doesn't prove anything. You could've easily driven back there last night after killing Sophia." Vance crossed his arms over his chest.

"And why lie about it?" I asked. My nerves had calmed down, and I found myself angry more than anything else. Angry that we had to sit here and listen to Lorraine's lies.

Amber's head bobbed back and forth between the conversations like a person watching a ping pong match.

Deputy Jones's eyes, on the other hand, never left Lorraine's face.

"Because I was meeting a potential client, okay? And I couldn't let Sophia find out about it. If she did, she'd fire me." Lorraine's eyes bore into mine.

"Who?" I asked, not backing down.

"Who was the client?" Lorraine asked. Her eyes darted out the window as she stalled for time.

I nodded. Of course, that's what I was asking. Lorraine wasn't going to be able to get out of it. Not without divulging her secret meeting anyway, if one had even taken place. At that point, I was betting it was fifty-fifty.

"I think you're going to have to come with us." Deputy Jones took two steps towards Lorraine.

Lorraine nervously licked her lips.

Deputy Jones reached for his handcuffs.

"Penelope Potions, okay!" Lorraine blurted out.

"I love her!" Amber clapped her hands.

"The influencer?" I asked.

Penelope Potions was all over social media. She rose to fame with a potent love potion mortals couldn't get enough of. In other words, she was a sellout. Most witches didn't take too kindly to others who sold our secrets for quick cash. We preferred to remain hidden, keeping our brooms in the cupboard, and thus us, safe. Every witching family has a tale of persecution. The witch trials didn't only take place in Salem. We took our secrecy seriously. Well, most of us anyway. Penelope Potions flaunted it.

"She's a witch ready for the prime time, ready to go public, and I'm going to take her there. Which is why I have to be going." The pitch in Lorraine's voice rose as she argued her case.

The deputies shared a look between each other.

"Look, I have a receipt from dinner last night, and you can call and speak with Penelope. She'll confirm I was with her. Oh! And the waitress was a fan. She'll remember us for sure."

I looked at Vance and bit my bottom lip. If Lorraine was telling the truth, she hadn't murdered Sophia. Not directly, anyhow.

"You got that number?" Deputy Jones asked.

"Yes, let me just find my purse." Lorraine looked at the ground beside her.

"I'll get it." I stood away from the table and walked out to the lobby where John had left Lorraine's luggage. Her purse was still sitting on the floor.

"Now what?" Vance said, following after me.

"I don't know. I was so sure it was Lorraine." I couldn't hide the frustration in my voice.

"Me too. But if she has an alibi—"

"I know." I didn't wait for Vance to finish his sentence. "And I turned her into a sloth," I muttered.

Vance smirked. "That you did." And then laughed, and the tension in the air broke.

I looked at the floor and shook my head, laughing

along with him. It was the first time I'd genuinely laughed in I don't know how long. I kept picturing Lorraine as a sloth with that dopey expression, and I'd laugh some more.

"Did you find it?" Deputy Jones came out to the lobby.

I was holding Lorraine's purse in my hand.

The deputy looked at Vance and me with our wide grins like we'd lost our minds.

"Sorry, yes, here you go." I handed the purse over.

Vance coughed and tried to regain his composure, but looking over at him, his laughter still showed in his eyes.

We waited out in the lobby for Deputy Jones to check on Lorraine's story. No sense in all of us standing awkwardly around the office. Plus, I still didn't trust Lorraine. Innocent or not, those claws of hers were deadly sharp.

It turned out we didn't have to stand around for long. Within fifteen minutes, Lorraine was free to go, and Amber walked past me, looking as smug as ever.

"Gosh, I don't like her," I replied as Amber's backside sashayed out the door.

"You never have," Vance remarked.

"That's not true. I tried to be her friend."

"When?" Vance didn't believe me for a minute.

"Kindergarten. Don't you remember? I shared my baby doll with her."

"And?"

"She ripped her head off."

"No, I don't remember." Vance laughed again.

I huffed out a sigh, but it lacked emotion. Amber was who she was. Nothing I said or did would ever change her. It was best to stay out of her way as much as possible.

"Should we get back to it then?" Vance didn't sound overly enthusiastic, and I didn't blame him. Not that I wanted an innocent woman to go to jail, but man, it would've been nice if Lorraine had been the bad guy.

CHAPTER FOURTEEN

I fell asleep sometime after three o'clock. At least that's the last time I'd looked at the clock. Both of our laptops were still open in front of us. Vance's forehead was down on his crossed arms on the desk, mirroring how I must've looked moments ago.

Sunlight filtered in through the front window blinds. I sat back and stretched, reaching my arms high above my head, and then turned my neck from side to side. I wasn't sure if it was stiff from sleeping with my head on the desk or from staring down at my computer screen half the night. Probably a combination of both.

Vance woke with a yawn. "What time is it?" He said at the same time, making the words sound like "whhhhha time is ittttt?"

Vance yawning made me yawn again, and neither one of us could speak for a minute. The phenomenon reminded me of a research article I'd read once about contagious yawning and empathy. The more you care about someone, the more likely you are to yawn after they do, and the quicker you are to do so. You had to love psychology.

After Vance and I finished yawning, I answered his question. "Almost eight." I looked down at my phone. No missed calls or texts. I wasn't sure if that was a good thing or not. I hadn't expected Aunt Thelma to check in, but it would've been a pleasant surprise if she had.

Vance rubbed his fingertips under his eyes as if wiping the sleep away.

"You don't have court, do you?"

"No, thank Merlin for that," Vance stood and stretched, placing his hands on his lower back and bending slightly backward. "But I do have to go to the office here." He stood up straight once more. "Did you find out anything else last night?"

I looked down at my notes. I'd gone through Sophia's production crew, well, what I could glean from her show's credits, and no one jumped out at me. If Aunt Thelma ever did call to check-in, I'd have her ask Arthur if he could think of anyone we should look into. Anyone who would be angry enough to follow Sophia out from California.

"Thelma, you here?" Benny's voice called from the lobby.

"Who's that?" Vance stood, cocking his head.

"The contractor. The one day he's on time." I stood and met the man and his crew out front.

"Hey, Benny."

"We've got the shower surrounds and toilets."

Benny hooked his thumb over his shoulder, motioning to the parking lot. "You should have working bathrooms by this evening."

My eyes widened in response, but I tried not to get my hopes up. Something could still go wrong. "That would be wonderful. Aunt Thelma's not here, but go ahead and get to work. We'll be sure to stay out of your way." I scribbled my cell phone number down on a sticky note behind the counter and handed it to the contractor. "I'll be in and out. Give me a call if you need me."

"Sure thing. Henry should be in after me with the rest of the carpet."

My day was getting brighter by the minute. "Really?" Even I could hear the optimism in my voice.

"He might have to work through the night, but you'll have your new carpet."

"Thanks, Benny." If only we could now do something about the tile, furniture, and finishing touches. One thing at a time, I reminded myself.

"I'm going to head out. What time's your meeting at Clemmie's?"

I turned in time to see Vance with his workbag over his shoulder.

"Ah... ten o'clock." I looked up and to the left while I recalled the time.

"Okay, I'll meet you there."

I opened my mouth to respond, but Vance didn't wait for my answer. My brow furrowed. He walked out the door. I had a feeling that was on purpose because

Vance didn't want me off wandering alone all day with a killer on the loose. And he hadn't wanted me to argue with him over it.

But he shouldn't have worried because *I* didn't want to be out wandering alone with a killer on the loose.

After getting cleaned up and tending to business around the inn, I headed out to Clemmie's shop, Sit for a Spell. Aunt Thelma had taken her car, so I was forced to walk. For the umpteenth time, I thought about getting a car. I transferred my wand from my purse to my jeans pocket, pulling down my shirt to cover the handle.

A breeze kicked across the lake, rustling the leaves and blowing waves ashore. I turned to my left and eyed the trailhead. It was a beautiful morning. The sun was out. The clouds looked light and fluffy—no reason to fear walking the trail.

Except it looked exactly the same yesterday. I shivered.

Fool me once, shame on you. Fool me twice, shame on me. I turned back toward the road and started walking the long way into town.

Now some might say I was a scaredy-cat. But me? I thought I was smart. I suppose I could transform into a cat and run down the Enchanted Trail into town, but that seemed even more foolish than walking like a sane person.

It took a bit longer, but soon Village Square was in my sights, as was Starry Evans. I turned my attention away from the news reporter and her growing crowd and headed toward the flagstone path that would take me to Clemmie's shop.

"There you are. Now, what in the world is going on?" Clemmie said when I walked in. The rest of the committee was already present.

"What do you mean?" I honestly wasn't sure what disaster they were referring to.

Clemmie gave me a level stare over her teapot. She was standing over Roger and Diane, ready to fill their cups. Even Misty eyed me over the rim of her cup, eyebrows raised.

"Morning, everyone," Vance said as he entered behind me.

Everyone turned their attention to Vance. Misty couldn't hide her Chesire Cat expression.

"Hey," I said to Vance over my shoulder as a welcome. I turned back around. Four sets of eyes stared back at us. "What?" I looked down to make sure I was properly dressed, and everything looked as it should.

"What is going on with you two?" Misty blurted out.

I turned back to Vance. He shrugged his shoulders, meaning he didn't know what Misty was talking about either.

"First you call off yesterday's meeting, then your aunt's car is missing, and then Vance stayed with you all night." Misty ticked the items off on her fingers, not at all bothering to downplay that last assumption. You had to love living in a small town.

I closed my eyes and shook my head. I realized how it looked, given Vance and my history, but last night had been entirely platonic. "It's not what you think," I started to say.

"Really? Because it looks like you blew us off for a little afternoon hanky panky, and Aunt Thelma left to give you some privacy," Clemmie smiled.

My mouth dropped open.

"Good for you," Roger quipped.

Vance coughed, forgetting how forward my friends could be. I held up my hands in a stopping motion. "Nothing like that happened."

"Well, I don't know what we were supposed to think," Diane muttered to Roger.

That got a smile out of me. I turned to Vance.

"Why don't you go ahead and fill them in," Vance pulled out a chair from a nearby table and sat down.

I copied him and took a steadying breath before plowing forward. "Yesterday afternoon, Aunt Thelma ran away with Arthur."

Diane and Clemmie gasped in unison.

"She did what now?" Misty asked.

"Why would she do such a thing?" Diane fidgeted with her pearl necklace. Even Roger seemed to sit up straighter.

I lifted my right leg placing my ankle on the opposite knee, my hands resting comfortably on my shin. "Aunt Thelma's convinced Arthur's innocent, and I am too. Well, for the most part."

"About that," Vance interrupted my explanation.

We all turned to face him.

"'The sheriff's officially charged Arthur with Sophia's murder. They're looking to bring him in."

The color drained from my face. "What evidence do they have?"

"I'm not sure yet. Deputy Jones is putting the case file together right now. I told him I needed the phone records as soon as possible."

I explained to everyone that Vance was representing Arthur, and we needed Sophia's phone records to trace a threatening call.

"So, where's the case at?" Diane asked, her voice thick with worry.

"Yeah, what do we know?" Roger chimed in.

"I'm going to kill her," Clemmie added. We looked at my aunt's best friend. "What? Thelma knows better than that."

I conceded the point.

Everyone's tea sat forgotten as they waited for me or Vance to continue.

"We figure someone killed Sophia Tuesday night," Vance started by saying.

"She was wearing the same outfit she'd worn the night before at dinner," I explained.

Vance nodded. "Right, and Percy saw her leave sometime after nine o'clock by herself."

"And nothing seemed off. Although, we all know how observant Percy is." I shrugged my shoulders. Percy was only as observant as he felt like being.

"Mm-hmm," Clemmie agreed with me.

"What about Arthur?" It was Diane who spoke up.

"He said he didn't see Sophia after he went to bed," I replied.

Roger cocked his head. His arms folded contemplatively across his chest as he leaned back in his chair.

I answered his unspoken question, "They're staying in separate, adjoining rooms. Arthur said he kept the door shut because he snores and Sophia didn't like it."

"Ah," Roger replied.

"Not sure if I buy that," Misty replied dryly.

"And you shouldn't. There's more to it. I talked to Arthur yesterday morning, and he admitted it wasn't a good marriage and was planning on moving back here. Alone."

"Really? Hm." Diane looked into her teacup before lifting it to her lips and taking a sip.

"What else you guys got?" Clemmie worked the room, refilling everyone's cups.

I looked to Vance to see if he wanted me to take the lead. He nodded in my direction. "Well, Misty and I overheard Rick Kelly threaten Sophia Tuesday night at the bookstore."

"Rick Kelly? Isn't he married to her niece?" Diane asked.

"Yes. We talked to Kayla yesterday. Stopped by to pay our respects," I started to say.

"And saw Rick." Misty's eyes went wide with meaning.

"Went that well, huh?" Clemmie sat down and sipped her tea. "Never did like that boy."

"Well, now I don't either." Rick's rudeness flashed through my thoughts. "But Rick didn't try to hide anything. Told us straight up how much he didn't like Sophia."

"Right before kicking us out," Misty said.

"No." Diane looked horrified. It was the worst sin in southern hospitality to kick someone out of your house, especially when that someone was paying their respects. Or, in our case, pretending to be.

"You don't think it's Rick then," Roger said pointedly.

I shook my head. "No. Not really. I had thought it was Lorraine."

"Who in the devil is Lorraine?" Clemmie asked.

"She was Sophia's business manager," I clarified.

"And she can't stand Arthur," Vance added.

"No, she can't. She also lied about when she got into town. She told us it was yesterday, but her luggage tags showed her flying into Atlanta Tuesday evening."

"We also discovered a key man insurance policy," Vance said.

"A what now?" Diane asked, teacup in hand.

"Don't look at me," Clemmie remarked.

"Isn't that when someone insures a key member of their business?" Misty supplied.

"It is. And Lorraine had a million-dollar policy on Sophia," I added.

"That's a lot of coin," Roger said.

"Does she get that money now?" Diane sat back.

"She might. I can't see why she wouldn't." Unless the policy had a murder clause or something obtuse.

Misty smacked the table and caused Diane to jump. "My money's on Lorraine then."

"Yeah, so was mine. But, she has an alibi," I confessed.

"One Deputy Jones confirmed. Lorraine wasn't even in Silverlake Tuesday night," Vance said.

"Where was she?" Misty wrinkled her brow.

"In Atlanta at a business meeting with Penelope Potions," I said.

"Gah! I can't stand that witch." Misty rolled her eyes.

"None of us can," Diane said dryly. By us, she meant every legitimate witch who worked to keep our craft secret.

"I don't know. I don't even know who she is," Roger said innocently enough. Diane patted his hand. It was the equivalent of saying, don't worry, I'll tell you about her later.

"Who does that leave then?" Clemmie asked.

"And you don't think it's Arthur?" Roger asked at the same time.

"Well, that's the thing. Arthur was acting off, but it was more like he was depressed, or maybe not depressed, but full of regret. I'm not sure." I tried to recall my lakeside conversation with Arthur, but I couldn't remember the exact words. "The takeaway I got was he felt like Sophia had taken advantage of him."

"She did that to everyone," Clemmie remarked, not the least bit surprised.

I gave Clemmie a sympathetic look. "I think Aunt Thelma was also starting to feel the same way."

"Which was why she ran off with Arthur then?" Clemmie tried to piece it together.

I thought for a moment. "Not exactly. I think Aunt Thelma did it because she knows what it's like to be wrongly accused and didn't want Arthur to have to go through that," I said.

Diane and Roger looked at one another. I'd forgotten they'd been previous suspects on another case, too.

Vance's cell phone rang, and he stood up to take the call, stepping outside in the process.

Diane, Roger, and Clemmie continued to talk to one another at their table. Misty leaned low toward me.

"So, you and Vance?" A wicked smile played across her lips.

"Nothing happened!" I hissed.

"You're keeping it private for now. I get it."

"Stop it. I'm serious. Nothing happened," but I smiled nonetheless.

"But you wanted it to, right?"

I swatted my friend's arm. "Speaking of which, how was your date last night."

Misty opened her mouth and then shut it.

"Oh, I see how it is. You can harass me, but you can't take a little heat."

"It's just that a witch doesn't kiss and tell." Misty mockingly turned her nose into the air.

"Since when?" I laughed.

So did Misty.

"Okay, it was a pretty magical first date. And some sparks might have flown. But we're taking it slow." Misty slowed down her pacing with the word.

I nodded. "Well, I'm happy for you. I like Peter."

Vance walked back in. "We've got those numbers."

That comment got our attention.

"Jones got the case file together quicker than I was expecting. I'm going to go pick it up."

"I'll go with you." I stood, leaving my full cup of tea on the table.

Vance nodded and walked back toward the door. I caught Misty's eye. She winked. I rolled mine in response.

"Call us. Let us know what you find out," Diane insisted.

"And if you see that aunt of yours, swat her upside her head," Clemmie added. I smiled my reply. I knew Clemmie wasn't serious. She was just concerned.

"What about the festival?" Roger asked, reminding us why we were all there in the first place.

I blinked.

"Right. Sorry. The festival. Did you all get the flyers?" I asked, searching everyone's face for their answer.

"We did. And we've got it all under control, don't we guys?" Misty gave everyone a level stare, daring someone to contradict her. "Go, if we need you, we'll call you." Misty smiled innocently at me. I knew full well it would take an emergency of catastrophic proportions before she would dial my number.

"Are you sure?" I wasn't one to skirt my responsibilities.

"Go, we're fine," this comment coming from Clemmie.

"Okay, you will call me if you need anything." I looked everyone in the eye, doing my best to show I meant business.

It didn't work.

"Sure, whatever you say." Misty's lips curved into that placating smile of hers. Everyone else nodded in false agreement.

I sighed and then took off with Vance out the door.

CHAPTER FIFTEEN

I waited in the truck while Vance ran inside and picked up the file from Deputy Jones. I didn't want to give Amber any reason to delay handing the case information off. Who knew what she might've come up with if she had seen me.

In less than five minutes, Vance was back in the truck with a slim manila file folder. He placed it on the seat between us.

"That's all they got?" I wasn't sure what I was expecting, but more than a few pieces of paper tucked into a folder, that's for sure.

"Looks like it," Vance remarked as he started the truck and put it into gear.

"Do you mind?" My hand had already reached for the file.

"Not at all." Vance looked left, then right, before pulling onto the street.

I picked up the folder and glanced at the first

page. It was a printout of Sophia's call log. I didn't recognize any of the numbers, but I did recognize the area code of a few. They were local numbers, and I was patient enough to wait until we were at Vance's office to use the internet to run a reverse phone number search.

I moved on to the next paper. My eyes skimmed the text. "What's this?" It was a rhetorical question. I re-read the first couple of lines. "Arthur filed for divorce?"

"He did?" Vance's attention snapped my way.

I held the piece of paper up for him to read. Vance could only take parting glances as he drove. Thankfully, his office wasn't far from the sheriff's department.

"Wonder if Sophia knew?" I asked, looking back down at the paper and turning it over to the next page to see if Sophia had formally responded, but no such documentation existed.

"Wonder if she found out and confronted Arthur on it. Then he got mad and killed her."

"Hey! I thought we didn't want Arthur to be the bad guy."

"I'm just saying how it could have played out. How the sheriff might see it."

"You might be right." I read the final document in the pile. It was an affidavit from Vicki Love, the same woman who worked for Misty at the bookstore. She witnessed Arthur and Sophia fighting on the Enchanted Trail Tuesday night around nine-thirty. According to the document, she had stayed late organizing the new releases when she overheard them on her way home. I relayed the message to Vance. "What do you think?"

"I think that paints Arthur in a new light, and I really want to look at that call log."

I grimaced. What if I'd misread Arthur and it wasn't grief that he was riddled with, but guilt? Surely, they could present the same. I twisted my hands nervously in my lap.

A minute later, Vance put the truck into park, and we wasted no timing heading inside his office.

Vance sat down at his desk, and I handed him the phone records. He placed the sheet of paper in front of him near his keyboard.

Leaning forward, I used my index finger to point to the one I was most interested in, tapping the series of numbers that called in between six-thirty and seven o'clock Tuesday night. "This is the person who threatened her. I'm sure of it." I straightened back up as Vance typed the phone number into a search engine.

A moment later, a set of results popped up on his screen. I couldn't help it. I leaned forward over Vance's shoulder again to read. But if we were hoping for a name to go with the number, we were both disappointed. All the results that popped up promised to uncover the caller for a fee.

"What does that mean?" I reread the scammy results.

"That whoever called Sophia blocked the call."

"So, we'll never know who threatened her?"

"No, we can find out, but it'll take time."

"But you just said it was blocked." I wasn't sure how anyone could uncover the number.

"The person blocked their caller ID, but the phone company can still trace it. Unless..."

"Unless what?"

"The person used a burner phone. A pre-paid phone that someone uses to commit a crime with," Vance quickly clarified at my confused expression. "But even those can be traced sometimes. Like if they used a credit card to buy it or activated it at home."

"Sounds like you know a lot about this stuff."

Vance shrugged. "It comes with the territory."

I looked back at the call log. "What about the rest of these?"

Vance put the numbers in one at a time. The out-of-state number turned out to belong to Lorraine. She called Sophia Tuesday morning and earlier in the week as well. Nothing suspicious about that.

Another one of the calls was from Arthur. Again, no surprise there. Even if they were getting a divorce, they'd still traveled to Silverlake together. "Plus, we know he didn't call and threaten her." He was sitting at the dinner table with me and Aunt Thelma.

"Who's that caller?" I pointed to four separate calls, all from the same number Monday through Tuesday.

Vance put the digits in the search box. "Kayla Kelly."

I tried to decide if that was suspicious or not. The two were family, and Kayla had already said Sophia visited her. The calls were probably the two of them making plans. "Do we have access to her text messages or email?" Maybe we could gain more insight there.

Vance ruffled through the papers. "Not yet. We're still in the discovery phase."

I stared off into space. "How can we get it?" I said more to myself than anyone. Was there a spell we could use? A way to hack into her email? "Do you know of anything?"

"We can try Arthur."

I gave Vance a look that said, "*Very funny.*" Shaking my head, I added, "Even if he wasn't on the run, I don't have his number."

"No, but you have your aunt's. Have you tried calling her?"

I blinked. "No, I didn't think there'd be a point." What was the point of running away if you were going to answer your phone? But Vance was right. I should at least try. I didn't wait for him to say anything else as I fetched my cell phone and dialed Aunt Thelma's number.

Two rings later, she picked up.

"You answered."

"I said we were taking a trip. Not disappearing off the face of the earth."

"Well, you could've said so."

"I thought I did."

I closed my eyes and fought to bring the conversation back on track. "Listen, couple things. One, Arthur's been charged with the murder. So don't even tell me where you're at." That way, I couldn't be charged with withholding information or whatever Amber could come up with. "And two, we're looking into Sophia's past. Is there anyone you or Arthur can think of we should check out?"

Aunt Thelma relayed the information to Arthur. I couldn't make out his comments. "No, dear, not that we can think of."

"No one?" I tried to keep the disappointment from my voice and failed miserably.

"We weren't really close with Sophia anymore."

"I see." Which made my last question all the more improbable "I don't suppose Arthur knew Sophia's email login?"

Aunt Thelma asked Arthur. "He said try Rich-Witch99. Capital R and W. Password money with a capital M and two dollar signs."

"What?" I hadn't expected a response. I snapped my fingers at Vance for a pen. I fumbled, taking the one from his offered hand, and scribbled the information down, reading it back to make sure I had it right.

"If not, he says try SuperStar for the password. Both S's capitalized," Aunt Thelma relayed.

"Is that Magic Mail?" I assumed that was Sophia's email provider. It was the one almost every supernatural used.

Aunt Thelma asked Arthur. She came back on the line, "Yep, Magic Mail. What's that?" Aunt Thelma was back to chatting with Arthur. "He says she never changed her passwords and she's probably still logged in on the home computer if it comes down to that."

"Does that mean you're in California? Wait, don't answer that. We'll check these out and see if they work."

Vance was already clicking ahead on his computer.

"We're in." His voice came from behind me.

"We're in?" I couldn't believe it. "It worked!" I said to Aunt Thelma.

"That's nice. Now you stay safe, and we'll see you soon."

"Wait!" I wanted to tell my aunt to be careful. That Arthur might be dangerous. That he could've killed Sophia. I wanted to tell her that I loved her and that she needed to be safe. I'd just gotten her back in my life. I wasn't about to lose her again. But the words went unspoken, and the line went dead.

I heaved a sigh.

"She'll be alright," Vance said, reading my mind.

I gave him a smile in return, but I knew the expression didn't quite reach my eyes. Instead, I turned my attention to Sophia's inbox. "Holy cats, she has a lot of emails."

"I know." Vance scrolled through, trying to sort what was relevant from the junk. Subject lines offering flash potion sales, buy one get one wands, and age-defying spells cluttered her inbox.

It took a bit to find something worthwhile.

"Look, right there. It's an email from Kayla."

Vance saw it at the same time and clicked on the message.

The email was from a couple of weeks ago, and it

started pleasant enough. Kayla asked how she and Arthur were doing, and she wondered if Sophia was coming to town. She had heard a rumor that Sophia would be here for the festival, and she was hoping they could catch up. Then she asked if her aunt was ready to "make things right."

"What do you think that means?" I asked.

"I'm not sure." The email ended with Kayla leaving her cell phone number and asking Sophia to get in touch with her. Vance clicked on Kayla's name and searched Sophia's email for more messages.

"Check the trash, too," I added, seeing what Vance was up to.

"Already on it." Vance did an email-wide search. Four additional emails popped up. All of which had been thrown away. Fortunately, Sophia never bothered to empty her digital trash, meaning we easily recovered them.

As we read through the emails, my expression turned from one of surprise to downright shock. "Kayla starts by asking for help."

"And ends with blackmailing her," Vance finished for me.

"Why, though? It was the same with Rick at the bookstore. Do they just want money?" I knew Vance didn't have the answer to my questions, but that didn't stop me from asking them.

"Rick said they knew she was a fake, right?" Vance recalled our earlier conversation.

"Right. Something along those lines."

"So should we assume that it was Kayla or Rick that called and threatened Sophia at dinner?"

"I think that's a safe bet."

Vance and I both looked at one another, wondering what our next move should be.

"You want to call it in?" Vance looked at me.

"I don't know. We were wrong last time. I don't want to get caught calling wolf. Right now, we know Kayla threatened Sophia, but that's it. I'd feel better talking to her first, feeling out the situation, and going from there." Plus, it was the middle of the day, and I wouldn't have to go over there alone.

"I can work with that. As Arthur's attorney, it's my job to check out other leads."

"So, you're good with going over there?"

"Let's see what she has to say."

Vance stood, and I gave him a weak smile. Suddenly I wasn't feeling as brave as I was five seconds ago. But time wasn't on our side, and the sooner we solved this mystery, the better off we'd all be.

CHAPTER SIXTEEN

I wasn't sure how this would go, and the fear of the unknown made me twitchy. My fingers drummed nervously on my knees as Vance drove to the apartment complex. He looked over at me out of the corner of his eye. He didn't say anything, but I stopped the tapping, clasping my hands in my lap instead.

I couldn't help it. This whole thing had me on edge.

If Rick was home, well, it wasn't going to be good. He wouldn't be happy to see me, and that was putting it mildly. We had already paid our condolences yesterday, and you can only win so many fake contests a week. Maybe I should've been crossing my fingers instead and hoping Rick would be at work and not home for lunch.

I exhaled.

"What's our plan?" Vance's eyes never left the road.

"I'm not sure. I think this time we're going to have to go with the truth." I motioned to the file folder on the seat between us. I'd printed off Kayla's email thread before leaving Vance's office.

"I think you're right. I don't see another way around it either."

Vance turned into the apartment parking lot, and my eyes started roaming the property.

Kayla wasn't at the park, which would've been nice. I would have loved to chat with her outside and preferably away from Rick. I double checked to make sure my wand was in my purse at the ready.

"Which one?" Vance nodded to the apartment blocks.

His question had me pulling my eyes from the playground and pointing out Kayla's unit.

Kayla answered the door with Ava on her hip. The baby happily suckled her pacifier and tugged her mama's hair. "Angelica." Ava tugged harder on Kayla's hair, making it harder for Kayla to say anything else for a moment. Kayla tried to pry her baby girl's death grip loose while still maintaining eye contact with us. Ava squealed with delight. The pacifier hit the ground and skidded across the tile entryway. Kayla bent down to retrieve it and, at the same time, asked, "Is everything okay?"

"Um, sort of. This is Vance Blackwell. He's your uncle's attorney and a friend of mine."

"Nice to meet you," Vance said and nodded at the introduction.

"We were hoping you had a moment to chat?" I asked.

"I do, but only a couple. Ava has a well visit with Constance in a half-hour." Kayla stepped back and allowed us entry.

I cautiously peeked around the tidy room, half expecting Rick to materialize, but he appeared to be out. But just to be on the safe side, I asked, "Is Rick here?"

"No, his crew started a new job today. Repaving a country road or something. Truthfully, I wasn't paying much attention when he was going on about it this morning. Ava's teething, and she's been keeping me up quite a bit." Kayla plopped Ava into a bouncer. The baby happily started jumping, causing the toys to rattle. I smiled at the little one before turning my attention to the file folder.

We followed Kayla over to the kitchen table and sat down. Ava was still in sight in her bouncer. Kayla made sure of that.

"I'm not sure if you heard, but the sheriff charged Arthur for Sophia's murder," I said, broaching the reason for our visit.

"Oh my gosh. That's awful. I don't know my uncle all that well, but I'd hate for it to be true," Kayla replied.

"As would we, which is why Vance and I have been looking into your aunt's correspondence." I turned to Vance, letting him take the lead, but Kayla didn't wait for him to.

"This is about those emails, isn't it?" Kayla stood and started fixing a bottle even though Ava wasn't fussy. I had a feeling it was more something to do to keep her busy and keep her nerves in check.

"It is. What can you tell us about them?" Vance asked.

Kayla paused while scooping powdered formula into the bottle. "Well, I figured the sheriff would come asking about them sooner or later, but I might as well tell you about it, too." Kayla was silent again while she shook the bottle for a minute, mixing the powdered formula with water, and walked it over to her daughter. Kayla walked back over to the kitchen, but instead of joining us, she got out a clean washcloth, wetted it under the faucet, and got to work wiping down her already clean countertops. While working, she said, "Sophia, God rest her soul, wasn't a good person. She stole those recipes, all those spells, from my mama and Granny. Granny said she didn't mind one bit because they were good spells, and she thought that what was good for Sophia would be good for the rest of us." Kayla looked up. Her expression showing how much that wasn't true. "But Sophia didn't look out for us. All she ever did was take from the family and never give back." Kayla rinsed her rag out, added more soap, and got to work scrubbing the front of her cupboards. "Sorry. I'm a nervous cleaner. It helps soothe my thoughts." Kayla shrugged, her cheeks turning pink.

"No, that's okay," I replied. "Do whatever you need to do."

Vance shrugged his shoulders like it didn't bother him in the least.

"Granny might've been fine with Sophia using her spells, but Mama wasn't. Sophia couldn't spell her way out of a paper sack, and here she was claiming to be an expert. I'm sure you saw that I asked her to make it right. Sophia eventually said she would, but when she stopped over, all she did is give me a check for five hundred dollars and a cease-and-desist letter from her lawyer. How is that making it right? My husband, he works hard for this family. He shouldn't have to. Not with the money Sophia stole from us." Kayla stopped cleaning and hung her head. "I wanted her to give us a cut in the royalties or acknowledge Mama or Granny's spells. Do something other than just steal it." Kayla shook her head and looked up. Tears pooled in the corners of her eyes. She left the washcloth on the counter and used the back of her hand to wipe them away.

After giving her a moment to compose herself, I said, "So what happened after that?"

Kayla shrugged her shoulders. "It got heated, but she left good and well." Kayla held up her hands in a surrender motion. "Honestly, I didn't put a spell on her anything. Although, I did think of a curse or two. But I bit my tongue. 'Course, Rick had a few things to say when he got home. He didn't like seeing me so upset." Kayla moved on to packing up the diaper bag.

"Did you call Sophia after she left?" Vance asked, hinting at the threatening call Sophia received at dinner.

Kayla didn't hesitate. "No. That was the last time I

talked to her, which makes me feel awful, but what can I do? It's something I'll have to live with for the rest of my life." Kayla's expression read true.

"Where were you Tuesday night?" I asked, as gently as possible.

"I know what you're thinking. I didn't kill her. Why would I? With Sophia gone, my family will never get the credit they deserve or see any of the money. There's no one to set things right. My hope died with her, and I'll tell the sheriff the same thing."

"But what about Rick?" Vance probed.

Kayla faltered, pausing with the diapers in hand. "W-w-what do you mean?"

"Could he have been mad enough to kill her?" he asked.

I raised my eyebrows. Could that have been the way it went down, and Rick wasn't even trying to hide it? I assumed he was innocent because only a fool wouldn't try and hide what they'd done, and Rick didn't seem like a fool. But I didn't know the man at all.

"I don't know." Kayla paused, then shook her head as if she didn't want to believe it. "No, he wouldn't do that." But her voice lacked conviction.

"Do you know where he was Tuesday night?" I asked.

"Uh... he worked late finishing a job. I'm not sure where. I thought he'd be home by the time we got back. I took Ava to family movie night at the community center," Kayla explained. "But he came home after I was in bed with the baby."

I gave Vance a knowing look. It sounded like Rick had plenty of time to kill Sophia before making it home with no one else the wiser.

On cue, Ava started fussing in her seat. "I'm sorry, but we really do have to get going." Kayla hiked the diaper bag over her shoulder and moved to pick Ava up.

Vance and I took it as our cue to leave, saying our goodbyes at the door and walking back to his truck.

"What's your impression?" Vance asked, starting the truck.

"That we better call Deputy Jones and tell him to take a good, hard look at Rick Kelly." I clicked my seat-belt in place.

"I couldn't have said it better myself."

CHAPTER SEVENTEEN

Vance wasted no time taking out his cell phone and calling Deputy Jones while pulling out of the apartment complex. I had no idea where we were headed off to, and I don't think Vance did either. We just needed to leave and not have Kayla see us sitting in her parking lot when she went to take Ava to the doctor. Neither one of us wanted to spook her more than she already was or tip-off her husband that we were on to him.

"Hey, Jones, it's Vance. Listen, Angie and I uncovered some evidence. You got a minute?" Vance hit the speaker button so that I could hear the deputy's conversation.

"How important is it?" the deputy asked. A beeping sound, the kind that a large truck makes while backing up, filtered in from the background.

Vance held the phone with his left hand up to his mouth, leaving it on speaker. "Well, we found out that

Kayla Kelly was blackmailing Sophia and the two women got into it Tuesday afternoon. Her husband Rick came home afterward, and he wasn't too happy. He's also unaccounted for Tuesday night." Vance let the implication hang in the air.

"Alright. In that case, you mind meeting me at the intersection of Church Street and Saint James?"

"Those are county roads," Vance remarked.

"You got it. I'm going to be out here for a while. Got a bit of a scene here, and the sheriff's with me, but I think he'd like to hear what you have to say."

I looked to Vance. I didn't like the sound of that, but what were we supposed to say? Vance looked hesitant too but replied, "We'll be there in about thirty minutes."

Vance hung up with the deputy and again met my gaze. Church Street and Saint James were outside of Silverlake, back in the everyday mortal world, which made it all the more odd that our sheriff was on the scene.

"What do you think's going on?" I asked, my voice not more than a whisper.

"I don't know, but it can't be good."

Uneasiness uncoiled in my belly and moved throughout my body with every beat of my heart. Vance was right, whatever had happened at the intersection of Church and Saint James wasn't good. Unfortunately for me, I had a very active imagination. I tried to steal my resolve for whatever we might be driving up to, but it was hard given the images from Tuesday morning. Sophia's body floated into my memory, and I shuddered.

A quarter-mile before the named intersection, we rolled up on a neon orange sign notifying us that road work was straight ahead. A convoy of county commissioned vehicles pulled off on the right-hand shoulder confirmed that. Vance slowed as we drew close. Mixed in with the asphalt truck, heavy-duty equipment, and regular pickup trucks were two deputy cars from Silverlake. Of course, a mortal would never know where they were from. The town's name had been charmed away, leaving them to look like regular county sheriff cars. The vehicle's emergency lights danced across the highway, reflecting off the work machinery.

Vance pulled up behind one of the unmarked pickup trucks and parked. Cautiously, I got out of the truck. My shoes crunched the gravel onto the dirt-packed shoulder. A couple of workers turned and watched us approach, open speculation clear on their faces. Their gaze lingered and made me feel self-conscious.

Thankfully, we are able to bypass the introductions and awkward small talk when Deputy Jones spotted us. He wordlessly motioned with two fingers for us to come closer. I politely smiled as I sidestepped the men and moved further down the road where Deputy Jones was waiting. We stood at the back end of his cruiser. Careful to stay on the shoulder of the road.

"It's Rick Kelly, isn't it?" I aired the suspicions I'd had from the moment I saw the construction road sign.

I wasn't sure what had happened, but I knew he had to be involved.

Deputy Jones nodded. "'Fraid so. Suicide." The deputy looked down at me from the top of his sunglasses.

I leaned forward, bracing myself against the back end of the car. Speechless, I didn't know what to say. Vance stood protectively next to me and rubbed my shoulder in a comforting gesture. I hadn't cared for Rick, but I didn't want anything bad to happen to him either. My first thought was of his poor wife and their baby girl. Kayla had no idea what life-altering news awaited her. I felt grief-stricken for her and knew I'd do whatever I could to help her in any way I could. I sucked in a shaky breath.

"Are you sure?" Vance asked.

"Left a note. He confessed to killing Sophia, too. Said he couldn't live with himself, and that was that."

My mouth dropped open in shock.

"He confessed?" I then turned to Vance. "So, we were right?"

"I guess so." The way Vance replied told me he didn't feel good about it. I had to agree. Rick's death was the worst way I've ever been proven right before in my life.

Vance motioned with his chin up the road. "How'd he do it?" His morbid curiosity getting the best of him.

I shook my head, not sure if I even wanted to know.

But Deputy Jones told us how anyway. "Overdose. Looks like he had a script from a previous work injury."

That wasn't hard to believe. Construction wasn't an easy job. There were dozens of ways to get injured on the site, not to mention the threat of cars hitting you. I instinctively inched further onto the shoulder of the road. Construction was backbreaking in the literal and figurative sense. "We'll check into it, but I expect it will pan out."

Neither Vance nor I had anything to say in response to that.

The deputy continued, "The sheriff has a couple of questions for you both, which is why I asked you to meet me down here." Deputy Jones motioned with his head to a pickup truck, two cars in front of us. We stood to the side while an unmarked ambulance approached. It took me all but a moment to realize that they were here to transport Rick's body, but still, it didn't make sense.

"How did they get here?" I pointed to the ambulance.

"We got lucky, and Rick's friend, Marty, found him and called us," Deputy Jones nodded his head toward one of the workers. The guy was more of a kid than an adult. The young man had dark hair and deep-tanned skin from spending his days working out in the sun. Although at the moment, Marty looked a little green in the face. He was sucking in air and puffing out his cheeks as he exhaled, looking anywhere but at Rick's truck. I vaguely recognized him from Silverlake, meaning he was a supernatural of some sort. I wanted to tell Marty that I understood the sick feeling and that it would pass, but I stayed rooted to the spot. "Easier and less spell work for everybody," Deputy Jones continued saying.

I opened my mouth to speak, but I wasn't sure what I would say, so I shut it instead. Deputy Jones's words rolled around in my brain like marbles. Easier and less spell work. Realization dawned, "You mean keeping the mortals out of it."

The deputy nodded. "What they don't know won't hurt them." Deputy Jones motioned to the sheriff, who had just finished saying something to the paramedics.

Sheriff Reynolds strutted over with an arrogant smirk that hadn't left his face in over twenty years—I was sure of it. Imagine if the varsity football team captain became the sheriff, and you pretty much have a picture of Sheriff Reynolds. It wasn't hard to see where Amber got her attitude from. The apple never fell far from the tree, even the poisonous ones.

"Amber said you were back in town playing detective. What, that hotel of your aunt's doesn't keep you busy enough?" The sheriff laughed at his joke.

I carefully kept my expression neutral, which was difficult. I would have loved nothing more than to snap back with, "Oh no, I have plenty to do, and maybe I could get back to it if you and your daughter could do her job." But the comment would've cost me dearly, and I didn't have time to sit in a holding cell.

"Good to see you, Sheriff," Vance thrust out his hand, his words interrupting my internal retort. It was probably a good thing.

Sheriff Reynolds shook Vance's hand and got right to it. "What's this I heard you interviewed my vic?" The sheriff turned his attention to me.

"I'm not sure I would so much call it an interview. I ran into Rick a couple of times this week. The first time was at the bookstore when he threatened Sophia. The second time was at his house when I was visiting Kayla."

"How'd that go?" Sheriff Reynolds looked down at me.

"Rick didn't appreciate my visit. Said Sophia had no business at his house either. He told me to leave." I shrugged my shoulders.

"And you didn't think you should report that to the sheriff's department?" Sheriff Reynolds looked at me like I was an idiot.

"My experience, Sir, is that the sheriff's department isn't always interested in my observations." I was careful to keep my voice respectful. My response was critical enough.

Sheriff Reynolds let that comment go. Probably because he knew I was right. Instead, he asked, "In any of these chats of yours, did you ever uncover a motive?"

I looked to Vance and let him answer the question thinking the less I talked, the better. "We did. I'm representing Arthur, and he told us that Kayla and Rick were blackmailing Sophia. We have the email thread to prove it."

I noticed how Vance didn't say that we had

accessed Sophia's email. I had a feeling that was a rather gray area with the law.

"Greed, that's what all this boils down to. People after the poor woman's money." Sheriff Reynold's scoffed.

"It's not just about the money. Sophia stole the spells from her family. Kayla wanted the recognition to go with them as well."

"So, let's just go on killing people over it now, shall we? You think Rick's actions are justified?" Sheriff Reynolds tucked his thumbs in his belt loops. His stance, wide.

"That's not what I meant." This time, my tone was defensive.

"Regardless of what you meant, the fact of the matter is Rick Kelly murdered Sophia, and now he's dead too. Those are the facts. Now I have two dead bodies and a ton of paperwork to do." Sheriff Reynolds sounded as if the paperwork was the worst of the two. "Do me a favor. Follow Deputy Jones back into town and sit with him so he can get your statement. I want to write down everything you said."

"I can do that." It was the first reasonable request I'd heard out of the sheriff or his daughter in I don't know how long.

The sheriff then turned his attention to Vance. "And you can let your client know that we'll no longer be pressing charges. Looks like we got an open and shut case here." The sheriff winked, rather pleased with the turn of events. "Just the way I like them."

"I'll pass the message on," Vince remarked, his voice even.

The sheriff nodded. "That's it then," and he turned, dismissing us.

I eyed Vance wearily, and together we walked back to his truck. I tried smiling encouragingly at Marty as we passed by, but the young man wouldn't meet my eyes. I looked over at Vance and shrugged as if saying, "*I tried*."

"C'mon, let's go," Vance motioned with his head, and I picked up my pace.

CHAPTER EIGHTEEN

Two hours later, Vance and I were leaving the sheriff's department. It probably should've only taken an hour, but Amber insisted on being present for the statement and found it necessary to question everything that I said.

The warmth from outside felt comfortable on my skin after sitting in the air-conditioned office for too long with nothing but a bottle of water to sip on. You would think Amber was interrogating us with the way she ran things. It would be great if she'd leave town and go play deputy someplace else. Silverlake only needed one Reynolds with a badge.

Eventually, Deputy Jones turned to Amber and said, "You know, I got this," signaling to her to back off. I smiled my thanks in response. I knew Deputy Jones had to walk a fine line with the sheriff's daughter, which made me appreciate his comment all the more.

"I know that look. What are you thinking? It can't

be good," Vance remarked as we walked over to his truck.

I smoothed my scowl. "A million different ways to curse Amber," I confessed.

"Ah, that would be a bad idea," Vance said, but he still smirked.

"Which is why I'm only thinking it." I mock sighed.

"You know what would be a good idea?"

"Huh?" I glanced over at him while walking.

"If we got something to eat."

I hadn't felt hungry until Vance said something, and then suddenly, I was starving. It was like my stomach hadn't been talking with my brain, but now it picked up the phone and dialed 911.

"Now that you mentioned it, I'm famished. Tavern?"

"Tavern." Vance was thinking the same thing I was —a hot meal and a cold drink was just what the day needed. The tavern was the place to go if you wanted good food and not a lot of fuss. The bar's technical name was Dragon's Mead, but most locals referred to it as the tavern. Guess that meant that I was back to being a local again.

As Vance drove, I realized that I hadn't even checked in with Benny, the contractor. It was a case where I was crossing my fingers that no news was good news. Something in the day had to go right. I shared my outlook with Vance after confirming I had no missed calls.

"There's hope yet," Vance turned to me with a smile.

"I really want this to go right," I confessed, looking out the window.

"Then it will."

I replied with a soft smile and looked back out the window, wishing I had the same confidence.

WE SAT with a couple of cold pints between us, waiting for our food to come out. Vance and I both starred off into space. It had been a long day. Heck, it had been a long night. Any time you fall asleep with your head on your desk was a long night. I mentally calculated just how little sleep we'd gotten the night before. The answer was not enough.

But once the shock of Rick's death wore off, I started to question it all. "Doesn't it seem a little off to you?"

"Everything about this week seems off." Vance lifted his beer to his lips and took a drink.

"True, but I meant with Rick. I didn't know him all that well, but suicide seems out of character." I thought some more, staring at my drink as the tiny bubbles rose to the surface. "I guess what I'm saying is, I can't see him going down without a fight."

"A firefight would've been more believable," Vance said, putting his drink down.

"Exactly. Rick didn't strike me as the kind of guy whose conscience would get the best of him."

"You think someone set it up to look like a suicide? Make him a fall guy?"

"It does wrap everything up nice and neat."

"Too neat?"

"That's what I'm wondering."

"Alright. I can buy that. But who?"

I looked at my draft. "I hate to say it, but what about Arthur? What does he gain from Sophia's death?"

"Good question. I didn't pull Sophia's insurance information yet, but the spouse is usually the beneficiary."

"And Sophia was probably worth quite a bit. So, money could be a motive," I conceded.

"Or Arthur could've just snapped on the Enchanted Trail."

"A murder committed in the heat of the moment." I leaned back and nodded my head.

"We know they were arguing, and Arthur had filed for divorce."

I took a deep breath. "Maybe we're overthinking things, and Rick really is the killer. Who cares if it's tied up nice and neat?"

Vance smirked. "You don't want Arthur to be the killer."

"No, I don't." I sat back against the booth, feeling dejected.

"Alright, I got two olive burgers here for you both with

curly fries." Bonnie, the co-owner of the tavern, or how she liked to introduce herself— Craig's better half, set our food down in front of us. She retrieved a bottle of ketchup from a pocket in her apron. "You guys need anything else?"

"No," I mumbled, unable to even feign a smile.

Vance wordlessly shook his head.

Bonnie frowned. "Now what's going on? You two seem upset. Anything I can do to help?" Bonnie propped her tray against her hip and leaned against the wooden-backed booth. Her gray hair was pulled back in a twist, and even though the tavern was busy, Bonnie looked like she had all the time in the world for us.

"We're just talking about Sophia," I said, nabbing a fry off my plate and munching on it.

"I know, shocking, isn't it? I told Craig I couldn't imagine such a thing happening here. And poor Arthur. You know I saw him here Tuesday night." Bonnie leaned forward as if imparting vital information.

Her comment got our attention.

"You did?" I cocked my head.

"You mean with Sophia," Vance clarified.

"No, he was with his sister, Connie. They sat here until almost eleven o'clock."

"Connie from the potions shop?" I remarked.

Bonnie nodded.

"I didn't know they were related," Vance said, taking the words right out of my mouth.

"Well, they are, and Arthur was pretty upset. I

didn't hear about what. I try not to eavesdrop, but there you have it."

Someone called Bonnie's name from over at the bar. She turned back to us, laying her hand on Vance's shoulder. "Let me know if you guys need anything else. I'll pop back and check on you in a couple of minutes."

"Thanks." I smiled at the woman as she turned to walk away. I looked at Vance with wide eyes.

"So let me see if I got this straight. Arthur told the deputies that he didn't see Sophia after he went to bed. Percy said he saw Sophia leave alone around nine o'clock, but we know from Vicki that Arthur and Sophia were arguing on the trail after that. Then Arthur was here at the bar until at least eleven."

I stared down at the table, picturing how it went down. The scenes played in my head like a movie. "Too bad Percy didn't see Arthur leave."

"Unless Arthur didn't go out the front door." Vance raised his eyebrows.

I sat up straight. "What did you say?"

"There's more than one door in and out of the inn. Arthur could've gone out any one of them."

"Or, he could've walked right out his room's patio door. Arthur had a lake view room with patio access."

Vance threw both his hands up in the air. "That's how he did it then. He didn't need to go out the front door."

"And why would he if he had just murdered his wife. He'd want to sneak in under the radar." I couldn't believe it. It all made sense. "Oh man, Vance. We need to track down Connie and see what she'll tell us before we go to the police."

"Do you think she'll talk to us?"

"Probably not, but we at least need to try. You know it's going to take a heck of a lot of evidence for the sheriff to look at anyone other than Rick."

Vance agreed with me. I could see it in his expression, but then something shifted. "Okay, but say Arthur killed Rick to make it look like suicide. How did he do it? Isn't he with Thelma right now?"

I twisted my lips while I thought. "You're right, but Arthur might not be working alone. What if he convinced Connie to do it? She's a potions master. She could make it look like an overdose. Heck, maybe it was even Connie's idea, and the two of them plotted it out right here!" I tapped my fingernail on the table. "Oh my gosh, Vance, it makes perfect sense. We need to uncover something solid to take to Deputy Jones. He's the best chance we've got at someone listening to us." I looked down at my phone to see what time it was. It was just after six o'clock. We had just enough time to eat and run into the potions store and hopefully catch Connie before it closed for the night. "Eat quick. We have a killer to catch. Possibly two." I leaned forward and took a hearty bite of my burger. It wouldn't do us any good sleuthing on an empty stomach.

CHAPTER NINETEEN

The festival committee must not have needed me because not only had no one called me, but several of the Village Square shops decorated their storefronts. Bales of hay, smiling scarecrows, and giant orange pumpkins popped up everywhere. I smiled as we walked past the bright, inviting displays. Even on the bad days, Silverlake really did feel like home. It's odd how the feeling snuck up on me like that.

"Are you smiling?" Vance looked over at me as if I might have a screw or two loose. I didn't blame him given the last twenty-four or so hours.

"Hmm?" I hadn't realized that I was, but Vance was right. I was—an odd expression for someone who was about to interview a murder suspect. "Just thinking how Silverlake grows on you," I confessed.

Vance looked around, taking in the shops and people milling about. "It does. It definitely does."

I changed the subject back to the task at hand.

"Here's what I'm thinking," I said as we made our way down the flagstone path back to the potions shop. "We tell Connie how worried we are about Arthur, lay out the case, only we fail to mention that we know she was with him Tuesday night."

"So, you want to set her up," Vance surmised.

"Basically. Although I think I worded it nicer." I smiled up at him.

"That you did. And I like the plan. Keep it simple."

Walking into Mix it Up! was an assault on the senses. My eyes were instantly drawn to the wall of cauldrons against the side wall. Gold, black, bronze—you name it. They came in every size, from ones as small as a cereal bowl to ones large enough to sit in. A plethora of plants grew against the opposite wall. Their vines snaking together into a jungle mix. A caution sign hung above, warning patrons to snip at their own risk. A pair of hand-held sheers hung on a silver chain beside the sign. The center aisles were chocked full of potion wares. The rows of stacked glass bottles rivaled the liquor bottle display at the busiest nightclub in Chicago.

A glass display case stood in the center of the shop. The rectangular case had four sides customers could walk around with a hollowed-out center where Connie usually stood, ringing customers up. Higher-end potions and specialized ingredients Connie personally prepared were displayed under the protective glass. Things like mandrake root harvested under a full moon, polished vampire fangs, and fresh eye of newt. Plenty of the potions cost a pretty penny, too, if you didn't have the time or skill to brew them yourself.

Tonight, Connie wasn't at her usual perch. A caldron stood in her place. The contents of the gold cauldron hissed as a steady stream of purple smoke rose to the surface. The tendrils disappeared into the atmosphere. The sight was mesmerizing. A glass eyedropper, like an inverted closed tulip, was suspended over the cauldron connected to a glass stem —the bulb, filled with a dazzling gold liquid. Second, by second, a drop descended into the basin below. A wand hovered parallel over the cauldron, swirling the air and stirring the contents below.

Like a moth to a flame, I drew closer. The smell of the potion was intoxicating. It was sweet—a combination of lavender and vanilla and something else I couldn't place. I wanted to bottle it. Bath in it. Spray it around my house like air freshener. I inhaled a deep breath and instantly yawned on the exhale.

"Sorry," I shook my head. Unsure where that had come from.

"That's okay." Vance yawned back. I couldn't tell if it was another case of contagious yawning or if the potion had the same effect on Vance as it had on me.

My eyelids felt heavy. They fluttered shut, and I would've loved nothing more than to curl up on the cold, tile floor for a nice evening nap.

"Step back," the woman's voice commanded.

I jumped and swayed. Connie's voice snapped me

out of it. Even Vance started at my side. We both turned around at the same time as if in slow motion.

"Sorry, I didn't mean to scare you, but if you take another whiff like that, you'll pass out stone cold on the floor all night, and then some.

"What is it?" I turned my head, watching a thick bubble rise to the surface and then slowly pop, emitting a beautiful but apparently dangerous gas in the process.

"Sleep of the Dead, or it will be once it's done." Connie held her breath and peered over the edge of the cauldron to check the potion's progress.

"Is it really?" Vance looked like he wanted to step closer and examine it for himself. I had to clamp down the urge to pull him back by the back of his shirt. "It's a tricky potion, isn't it?" Vance's voice still held a note of wonder.

"Usually. I offer up a watered-down version in my new book, I don't need anybody accidentally killing themselves, but this right here is the real deal."

I took a step back, noticing the warning sign posted on the counter for the first time.

Connie followed my eyes. "I try not to brew it at the store but couldn't help it. The hospital needs more."

"For what?" I cocked my head.

"Surgery and sedation. I usually have a decent supply on hand, but someone broke in and stole it a couple nights ago."

"Any idea who?" Vance asked.

"Not a clue, and it's an odd target. I have far more valuable potions here." Connie explained at our confused expressions. "I've never felt the need to ward the place, but I'm rethinking that now, what with everything that's been happening." Connie's brow creased with worry.

"That's actually what we came in to talk to you about," Vance said.

I picked up Vance's segway, "Your brother's run off with my aunt, and I'm worried about them."

Connie closed her eyes and sighed.

I looked to Vance. I wasn't sure if her expression was a good thing or not. Vance shrugged his shoulders.

"I told him not to do it." Connie pinched the bridge of her nose and shook her head as if she couldn't believe it.

"Do what exactly?" Vance asked cautiously.

I leaned forward. Was Connie going to confess on Arthur's behalf?

"Run off, of course. I told him it would make him look guilty. But he didn't listen. I mean, he knew what people would think. They were going through a divorce, and they got into a fight Tuesday night, which Arthur lied about. I told him that was foolish too. Someone had to have heard them—this is Silverlake— and surely, they would tell the sheriff. Then Arthur would look even guiltier." Connie huffed.

And she was right. Somebody had overheard the argument and reported it. I kept that information to myself. "Speaking of which, do you know what they were fighting about?" I asked instead.

"About me." Connie pointed to herself. "Sophia and

I never got along. Arthur always had to sneak around to visit. It was easier to do that rather than have her cause trouble. And Sophia loved trouble, which is why she started fighting with Arthur. Hated that she couldn't cut me out of his life." Connie huffed. "I know you shouldn't speak ill of the dead, but that's going to take some getting used to. Sophia lied more than she told the truth. Which is where this came in." Connie walked behind the counter and slid back the glass-faced cabinet, pulling out a potion. "I always told Arthur he was under her spell, and it turned out I was right." Connie held up a vial of silvery blue liquid. The contents swirled inside like a storm cloud blowing in a rainstorm. Connie held it out for me to take.

"What is this?" I held the vile close to my face, examining the contents before passing it off to Vance.

"Apli Alitheia, otherwise known as Simple Truth," Connie replied.

"A truth serum," Vance remarked.

"I convinced Arthur to try a few drops last month, and POOF! He started to see Sophia for who she truly was. He filed for divorce shortly after." Connie shrugged her shoulders.

"Did Sophia know about the potion?" I asked even though my eyes were still glued to the vial in Vance's hand.

"Not that I know of. She never confronted me. And now that she's dead, any remnants of her spell would've been broken, which is exactly what happened. Her death hit Arthur like a slap in the face, making him realize just how much she manipulated him. A lot of people are probably feeling that way right about now."

I immediately thought of Aunt Thelma. Sophia must've had her under a spell as well. It would explain why she felt so indifferent to her friend's passing. And hadn't Diane suspected as much when Sophia stole her pie recipe, and Aunt Thelma refused to acknowledge it?

"Not that any of it matters now. I heard Rick Kelly confessed to killing Sophia." Connie took the vile back from Vance and tucked it safely back in the display case. "It's awful how it all went down. I feel bad for Kayla. She's a sweet girl. And their baby is such a doll."

"That she is," I remarked, watching Connie adjust the potions in the display case.

"You know, Rick was just in here the night before last. I can't believe it." Connie stood. "I was alone in here with a murderer. I'd like to think I'm a pretty smart when comes to potions, but give me a wand and I'm useless." Connie crossed her arms and rubbed her shoulders. "I've never given much thought to how I would defend myself. Never had to until now."

"Yeah, it's upsetting. I wonder how Kayla's holding up." I knew she didn't have any family in town. I should stop by and see what I could do. Maybe watch Ava so Kayla could rest or tackle whatever she needed to get done. I couldn't imagine the plans that she had to make or the decisions that lay before her.

"It's got to be hard for her. I was going to drop off a

calming potion. It won't erase her grief, but it should help her sleep and think straight. It's the least I can do."

"We can drop it off," I offered. "I was going to stop by and see her anyway," I decided on the spot.

Vance agreed it was a good idea.

"Let me package it up for you." Connie's fingers danced across the glass countertop, moving down until she landed on the potion she wanted. She pulled out a slim glass vial, only about three inches tall, with a cork stopper. The brew inside was pearlescent white. Even the look of it was soothing.

"The one thing I don't understand is why did Rick do it? No one seems to know," Connie said as she separated the top from the bottom of a small black box, tucking the potion into the ivory satin pillow below before closing the package.

"Kayla said she'd wanted Sophia to give credit to her family and a cut of the royalties. It sounded like when Sophia refused, Rick lost his temper. The whole situation is awful." I took the package from Connie.

"That it is. The poor girl has experienced far too much grief lately with the loss of loved ones," Connie remarked.

"I know. And now she's lost her chance at reconciliation with her aunt, too"

"Maybe personally, but not financially."

"What do you mean?" Vance asked.

"Kayla inherits everything. It's a family trust. A Saxe family trust. That's Sophia's maiden name. Old Miss Saxe made sure of that," Connie remarked.

"Kayla's granny?" I asked.

"That's the one. Miss Saxe wanted to make sure her family was provided for. That's what Arthur said."

I shook my head. "I don't think Kayla knows that."

"Maybe she doesn't. Arthur just told me about it when we were discussing the divorce Tuesday night. Sophia wanted him to reconsider, told him he would never see a cent if he divorced her, and he told her that he didn't care. That he'd rather be broke than be married to her."

"Ouch," Vance chimed in.

"Yeah." Connie sighed. "He was done with her, and I was proud of him standing up for himself. If only Sophia hadn't died the way she did. I do feel bad for the woman. No one deserved her fate." Connie looked off in the distance. "I only hope with Rick's confession that Arthur can now come home and put the pieces of his life back together. That's all I want for him." Connie looked as if she were about to cry. "Sorry," she turned and sniffed. "It's been hard."

Connie didn't just mean this week.

"I'm sorry." I rubbed her arm." I wish that for him as well."

"Well," Connie said, leaving the past in the past. From the way she said the word, I could tell that conversation was over. "Give Kayla my condolences, and tell her I'm thinking of her."

"Will do, thanks," I replied.

Vance added his goodbye, and we walked out of the shop into the evening air.

"Well, that was interesting." The potion gift bag swung in Vance's hand like a pendulum.

"Not exactly how I planned on that going down," I added as we walked back to Vance's truck. "Maybe we were wrong, and it is all neat and tied up, and we need to quit looking for something that isn't there.

"You might be right."

But even as Vance agreed with me, it didn't *feel* right. And there in lay the problem. If I had learned anything the last couple of months, it was to trust my instincts, and my instincts were telling me to keep on digging.

CHAPTER TWENTY

A moving van at an apartment complex isn't all that unusual, but when we pulled into the parking lot and saw that the truck was backed up to Kayla's apartment, now that was unusual.

I acted quickly, smacking Vance on the arm, not even thinking. "Go to the right," I hissed, using my right hand to point out my window.

In a split second, Vance did just that, changing his planned direction, turning away from Kayla's building, and driving down two more units to the opposite end of the complex.

"Things just got more interesting," Vance remarked, parking his truck and killing the lights.

"You can say that again. Why is Kayla running?"

"Maybe because she's the one that killed Sophia and set Rick up to be the fall guy?"

My mouth hung open. I couldn't believe it. I didn't want to believe it. Kayla had seemed like such a sweet girl. I didn't want to think she was capable of a double homicide, but something had to account for her skipping town.

"I'm going in." My fingertips were already around the tiger eye pendant hanging around my neck. In less than five seconds, I could transform into a cat and dash to the apartment.

"No, you're not." Vance looked at me as if I was crazy. "You're not confronting her. We're going to call Deputy Jones." Vance took his cell phone out to place the call.

"Call him, but I'm not waiting for him to get here. We don't have time." The truck was running, ready to pull away any moment. "Trust me, Kayla will never recognize me. Let me scope it out and see what's going on." I opened the truck door, and the spell was on my lips when a man's voice reached our ears.

"Get moving, Kayla! We got to get out of here." Rick strutted toward the van, yanked the door open, and climbed behind the wheel.

I was too shocked to speak. My heart hammered in my chest. I cleared my throat. "That's Rick Kelly," I said to Vance as if he didn't already know. "I thought he was dead."

"Didn't we all."

"Hurry up," Rick hollered back, trying to keep his voice low, but it still carried across the parking lot, bouncing off the handful of cars that separated us.

"I have to get Ava's things," Kayla replied from the doorway.

"Forget the baby crap. Just grab the kid and get in the van."

Even from this far away, I saw Kayla flinch as if Rick had struck her. It was abundantly clear—she wasn't a part of his plan. Kayla was as much a victim as Sophia had been. I turned to Vance. "We have to help her."

"I'm calling Deputy Jones now." Vance's fingers flew across his cell phone while he spoke.

"I'm going to transform and run back, see if I can get Kayla's attention. Get her and Ava to sneak back with me. We can hide out in your truck until Jones gets here." Vance wanted to object, I could read it on his face, but he knew it was a smart plan. Our only plan.

Vance replied with a curt nod. "I'll keep an eye on Rick."

"Okay, I'll be as quick as possible."

I took a calming breath, blocking out the chaos, and closed my eyes. In anticipation, the pendant grew warm against my chest. I pinched it between my fingers, inhaling confidence and exhaling the spell, "Metamorfóno alithís ousía." I felt the magic move through me. A slow tingle first until it burst through my body like an electric pulse—fast and hot. A heartbeat later, my four feet were on the pavement and I was covered head to tail in fur. Vance reached over and shut the door as I scampered off, disappearing into the surrounding shrubbery.

I was confident that Rick wouldn't pay any attention to a stray cat. But still, I didn't want any residents to happen upon me either and scoop me up to rescue me, something that had happened on a recent occasion. My soft feet pounded into the dirt as I sprinted, all four feet coming off the ground in rhythm. One side of me brushed up against the apartment building's brick base while the other ran against the bushes. Evergreen scratched at my fur but didn't bother me. I was moving too fast, with the mission in sight. Tucked safely behind Kayla's apartment building, I said the reversal spell and turned myself back into my human form. Thankfully, I had learned how to pull clothes into my shift, or else the rest of the evening would be mighty embarrassing. I cautiously peered into Kayla's sliding glass door and knocked on the window. My knuckles made a hollow sound against the glass.

Kayla jumped. Her head whipped toward where I stood.

I waved encouragingly.

Kayla cautiously slid open the glass door. Even in her ordeal, she still tried to sound polite. "I'm sorry, Angelica, but now is not a good time for company." Never mind the fact that I had snuck into her backyard and knocked on her patio door.

"I saw Rick. Come with us. Vance is with me." I waved Kayla forward.

Ava screeched from her high chair. Kayla looked back to her daughter then to me once more. When our eyes met the second time, they had tears in them. Kayla shook her head. "I can't. He said he'll kill Ava if I try to run."

I opened my mouth ready to reply, having expected Kayla to object, but shut it at her words. I figured Rick would threaten Kayla, but his baby? What was wrong with the man. I knew he was a murderer, but still. His words sickened me.

"I'm sorry, but I have to go. I've already taken too long."

"Deputy Jones is on his way. He'll be here any minute." The words rushed out as Kayla moved to shut the sliding door.

"Woman! Who are you talking to?" Rick's voice bellowed from the front door.

The fear in Kayla's eyes caused my heart to jump up into my throat.

Thankfully my feline instincts kicked in, and I clutched my tiger eye once more, instantly transforming into my feline alter ego.

Kayla blinked in shock, witnessing the transformation. "I-I-I," Kayla stammered, no doubt her mind raced to come up with an answer. "I thought someone was out here, but it's only a cat." Technically she wasn't lying.

"Get moving. They're going to realize my body's missing any minute now. Someone's bound to come calling," Rick rushed Kayla.

Kayla pulled the sliding door shut, blocking off the rest of the conversation.

I ran back around out front, ready to jump in Vance's truck and have him follow Rick until Deputy Jones could intercept, and froze. My front left paw was stuck in mid stride.

"What do you think you're doing?" Rick snapped. It looked like he caught Vance red-handed as he attempted to swipe the moving van's keys. It would've been a brilliant move if Rick hadn't seen him.

Vance moved for his wand, but Rick was faster with a gun.

My heart plummeted to my furry feet where apparently my courage resided because in that next instant, I screamed, which came out as a feral cry.

And like a feral cat, I charged fearlessly ahead. The sight of me barreling forward distracted Rick long enough for Vance to lunge at Rick, twisting his hand in an attempt to free the gun.

But Rick was strong, and before that moment, I hadn't realized just how much. His hand turned into a paw. Gray fur sprouted up around him. The air shimmered. And instinctively, I veered off to the side.

I assumed Rick was a witch. It was a mistake I wouldn't make again. Vance too recognized the error of his ways, but he was trapped. The massive wolf snapped and snarled. I was useless against the beast. But Vance didn't back down. He held his wand out before him, never breaking eye contact with the four-legged beast.

Time stopped.

I was terrified of what would happen when Rick attacked.

My heart hammered madly in my chest.

Then, a loud whistle punctured the nighttime air. We all looked over to find Kayla standing in the doorway, a pistol in her hand. She aimed the gun straight at Rick. He turned, realizing what she was about to do, and crouched down to spring in her direction.

Rick didn't wait. He leapt into the air toward his wife.

Kayla didn't flinch as she fired off one perfectly placed round. The bullet struck Rick in his chest. In an instant, the beast tripped over his front paws and skidded to a halt in the front yard.

Sirens wailed in the distance.

Kayla dropped the gun and stepped backward until her heels hit the doorjamb. She sank to her haunches.

I rushed forward, still in cat form, but transformed the moment I reached her, wrapping my arms around her shoulders.

"You saved our lives. You saved all our lives." My voice shook with emotion. I couldn't even process everything that had just happened, but one thing was for certain, Kayla was a hero.

Vance bent low over Rick, examining him. "You didn't kill him," he sounded as surprised as I felt.

"What?" I looked to Kayla to confirm.

"No," Kayla looked down at the gun. "It's a tranquilizer gun. My mama bought it for me right before she died. She never did like Rick."

Ava squealed from behind us. She still sat in her high chair, banging her bottle on the tray before her.

"It's going to be okay. It's all going to be okay," I said to Kayla and Vance as much as to myself. And for the first time, in a long time, I believed it.

CHAPTER TWENTY-ONE

"I didn't know about the trust until tonight." We were in Kayla's kitchen. Ava was asleep upstairs in her crib. I'd made Kayla a cup of tea with Connie's calming potion, and she was talking to Deputy Jones with Vance and me at her side. "Mama probably didn't tell me because she didn't want Rick to find out."

"She knew what he was really like," I said.

"She did even though I didn't tell her the half of it." Kayla's lips formed a thin line. I could tell she was disappointed with herself for the choices she'd made, just like I could tell that she wouldn't make those same choices again. "Rick called me an idiot when he found out about the trust. Couldn't believe I didn't know about it." Kayla looked down into her teacup. I imagined it was one of the many insults Rick threw her way during their relationship. "Guess he found out about it when he started looking into Sophia's finances. He wanted to see how much she was worth."

"And when he discovered it, he decided to kill her?" Deputy Jones asked.

"When blackmail didn't work. I swear, I didn't know anything he'd planned. He told me tonight he'd roped poor Marty into it too," Kayla shook her head in disbelief.

"The kid on the road crew?" I thought of the young man who'd looked rather green on the side of the road.

Kayla nodded solemnly.

"He's already down at the station," Deputy Jones said. "Rick got him to call the suicide in and bail him out of the morgue," the deputy added when I opened my mouth to ask.

"So, Rick had help pulling his stunt off," Vance said.

"And it turns out Marty's conscience was worth more than a couple hundred bucks," the deputy remarked.

"I about fell over dead myself when Rick walked in the door." Kayla placed her hand over her heart.

I could only imagine the shock she'd experienced.

"I couldn't understand what had happened and how Rick was standing before me. Sheriff Reynolds had left not more than an hour before."

"He used Sleep of the Dead, didn't he?" I took a guess.

Deputy Jones snapped his attention my way. "How'd you know?"

"Connie said someone stole her supply from the store and that Rick had been by," I replied.

"Did she now?" Deputy Jones thought about it.

"That's where he probably got it from then."

"I'm just so sorry you all got dragged into this." A tear slipped down Kayla's cheek.

"Listen, none of this is your fault. You drink up your tea, and if you'd like, I'll stay with you tonight." I had a feeling that was the reason Kayla's tea mainly sat untouched. She didn't want to drink a potion and not be able to tend to Ava.

"I couldn't ask you to do that," Kayla replied even though I could tell she wanted to accept my offer, which is why I pushed her a little bit.

"You didn't. I'm offering. Unless you'd like to stay at Mystic Inn?" I inwardly groaned. That was another problem. I had no idea how far along the inn was at the moment. I'd probably have to start making phone calls and canceling reservations in the morning. I tried to remind myself that it wasn't a big deal in the grand scheme of life, but it still made me feel like a big fat failure.

In the end, Kayla agreed that Ava would probably sleep best at home in her crib and accepted my offer to stay. Within ten minutes, Kayla drank her calming tea, and the effects started to work their magic.

"Let's get you settled for the night, and I'll stay on baby duty, I promise," I led Kayla upstairs to her room.

Kayla smiled her thanks and willingly allowed me to tuck her in. Kayla was a strong woman, no doubt about that, but sometimes it was nice to let someone take care of you for a change. I was more than happy to be that someone for her that night.

Vance was waiting for me downstairs when I came back down a few minutes later. Kayla hadn't even put pajamas on. She'd fallen asleep the moment she laid down.

"You're pretty amazing, you know that?" Vance said as I rounded the last step.

"Stop it," I looked down, not meeting his eyes.

"No, really. Silverlake is lucky to have you, and I'm just happy you're home."

At that comment I did look up. Vance smiled at me. I felt his sincerity from the crown of my head to the tips of my toes.

I changed the subject because what could I say in response to that? What should I say? I wasn't sure. "Thanks. For everything. I'll talk to you tomorrow?"

"Absolutely."

I walked Vance to the door and saw him out, watching him disappear down the sidewalk to his truck. Yep, we had history all right, and sometimes, like right at that moment, I wished we could have a future.

THE FOLLOWING day Kayla woke up with energy to spare. I, on the other hand, felt rough. Kayla hadn't been kidding when she said Ava was teething. The poor babe didn't sleep longer than an hour at a time, and then only when I held her. My arms were sore and my eyes were heavy. Two poor nights of sleep in a row had caught up with me, and I wouldn't make it through the day without copious amounts of coffee or a nap, maybe both. But it was worth it seeing Kayla smile.

"Thank you again so much," she said as she made a pot of coffee.

The aroma of the coffee filled the small space and had me longing for a cup right then and there. I would have loved to visit with Kayla for a bit more, but I had to get back to Mystic Inn and cancel the incoming reservations. I only wondered if a refund and a free-night stay were enough to compensate disappointed guests.

My phone chimed on the counter. I was about to call John for a cab ride when I saw a text from Vance. "Need a lift?" it read.

My fingers hovered over the keys while I debated what to reply. Old Angelica would say no and still call John. New Angelica would reply yes. So that is what I wrote back.

Vance arrived within ten minutes. I tried not to groan at how put together he was with his business attire while I was still in yesterday's clothes, in dire need of a shower and a toothbrush.

Bless his heart, if Vance thought I looked like a hot mess, he didn't say anything.

"Thanks for the ride. I've got a ton of work to do," I said, climbing into the truck. Vance listened silently to my plan. How I would call everyone, offer the refunds and free nights, and hope for the best. I was still worried about how upset guests would be and how it would all shake out, not to mention how disappointed the festival committee would be with the lower turnout. After all, why would visitors make the drive for the festival if there wasn't any place to stay? I made a mental note to call the mayor of Harrisville, being a witch, maybe he'd be sympathetic to our cause and give our visitors a deal. It was hard to say if he'd help, seeing I'd never met the man, but one could hope.

I was still stressing about everything like usual when we pulled into the inn's parking lot. I started counting the cars in the lot, recognizing quite a few of them.

"What's going on?" I turned to Vance, waiting for him to explain.

He didn't speak until he put the car into park. "Just a couple of friends who wanted to say thank you."

"Thank you?" I wasn't following.

"You do so much for Silverlake. We wanted to do something nice for you."

I got out of the truck and walked to the inn's front entrance, unsure of what I'd find inside.

What I saw took my breath away.

"It's beautiful," I said after walking in through the front doors.

The tile floor shined, the wood accents gleamed, and everything felt bright and new.

"Is that granite?" I asked, running my hand down the smooth surface of the registration desk.

Vance nodded that it was. He was silent, letting me take in everything.

"I can't believe you guys did all of this."

I walked down the hallway toward the guest rooms, wondering what else I'd find inside.

Stepping into the first open door, I froze.

"SURPRISE!" My friends shouted.

It was the best surprise of my life.

Aunt Thelma, Arthur, Misty, Clemmie, Diane, and Roger all stood bundled together with broad smiles on their faces.

"All the rooms are done," Diane said proudly.

"All of them?" I blinked in shock. The lobby was good enough.

"Every last one," Roger confirmed.

"And they're gorgeous," Aunt Thelma agreed, rushing forward to wrap me in a hug.

"You guys, I can't believe it." I said over my aunt's shoulder. I didn't know what else to say.

"Benny did most of the work," Aunt Thelma added. "But we came in and finished everything off."

My friends looked wearily to one another. I could only imagine how long they'd worked last night.

"I don't know how to thank you." I truly didn't.

"You being back home is thanks enough." Aunt Thelma held me at arms length.

And me, being one never to cry, freely let the tears fall. Yes, it was good being back home. I never planned on leaving again.

That night as the festal kicked off and the tourists rolled in, my heart swelled with pride with how everything had come together. Sure, there had been a few twists and turns along the way, but I knew that whatever life threw at me, I'd have friends and family by my side, and we'd get through it together. At the end of the day, that was all a witch could ask for.

READY FOR ANGELICA'S next mystery?

Halloween hijinx abound in Silverlake this year, keeping Angelica on her toes, and making this a spooky night no one will ever forget.

Available Here:

https://books2read.com/u/m2RaLd

Stephanie Damore Complete Works

Mystic Inn Mysteries

Witchy Reservations
Eerie Check In
Spooked Solid
Untimely Departure

SPIRITED SWEETS MYSTERIES
Bittersweet Betrayal
Decadent Demise
Red Velvet Revenge
Sugared Suspect

WITCH IN TIME
Better Witch Next Time
Play for Time

BEAUTY SECRETS SERIES
Makeup & Murder
Kiss & Makeup
Eyeliner & Alibis
Pedicures & Prejudice
Beauty & Bloodshed
Charm & Deception

A DROP DEAD *Famous Cozy Mystery*
Mourning After

SPIRITED SWEETS MYSTERIES

My name's Claire London and I see dead people.

Just don't tell anyone else or they'll think I'm crazy.

Er...I mean crazier.

My life was beautifully simple.

And then my husband died.

Bit of a shock when his ghost popped up.

Now there are other ghosts who need my help. I'll do whatever it takes to get them up to the Pearly Gates... and out of my bakery.

If you love a clean paranormal mystery, heavy on the whodunit, you're going to love these quick reads!

Bittersweet Betrayal

ABOUT THE AUTHOR

Stephanie Damore is a USA Today bestselling mystery author with a soft spot for magic and romance, too. She loves being on the beach, has a strong affinity for the color pink (especially in diamonds and champagne), and, not to brag, but chocolate and her are in a pretty serious relationship.

Her books are fun and fearless, and feature smart and sassy sleuths. If you love books with a dash of romance and twist of whodunit, you're going to love her work!

For information on new releases and fun giveaways, visit her Facebook group at https://www. facebook.com/stephdamoreauthor/

facebook.com/stephdamoreauthor

twitter.com/stephdamore

instagram.com/steph_damore_author